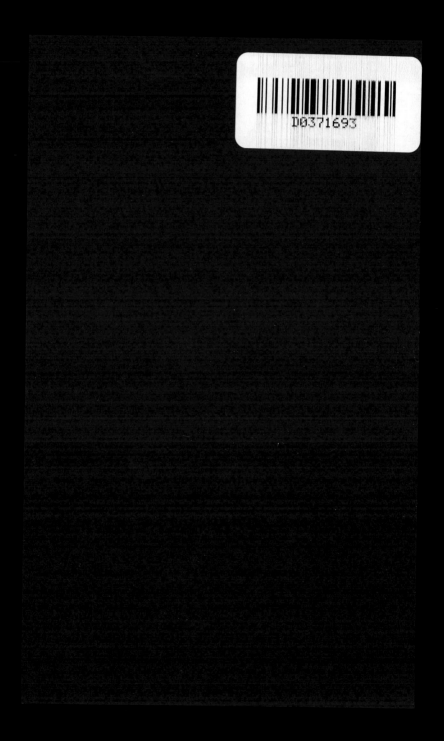
D0371693

4

SONS
OF THE
DARK

night Sun

Also in the

SONS OF THE DARK

series

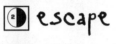

SONS OF THE DARK

night sun

LYNNE EWING

VOLO

HYPERION/NEW YORK

First Edition
1 3 5 7 9 10 8 6 4 2
Printed in the United States of America

Library of Congress Cataloging-in-Publication Data on file
ISBN 0-7868-1814-X

Visit www.volobooks.com

For Maggie

1000 B.C.

Yaolt climbed the stone steps toward the summit of the pyramid. For the past year he had played the role of his god Tezcatlipoca, anticipating this day. The flowers strung around his neck scented the hot tropical air, and the seashells tethered to his arms and legs clattered noisily.

The eight Toltec warriors, who had until this day been his attendants, now marched beside him as his guards, ready to seize Yaolt and drag him to the waiting priests. In the past, others had tried to escape. Some had even fainted and had to be carried to the altar in shame, but Yaolt intended to prove himself worthy of sacrifice. He was the chosen one.

He paused to smash a clay flute beneath his foot, just as he had done at each previous step. A fragment cut into his heel and broke off under the skin. The pain didn't stop him; he crushed the next flute with an unrestrained stomp.

Praise for his courage rose from the crowd below. Every broken piece of pottery meant another blessing for his people, and he planned to give them good fortune before he died.

When he reached the summit, five priests escorted him to the altar. Yaolt didn't struggle or plead for his life as he had seen others do. Instead, he bent backward over the jutting rock until his chest arched toward the heavens. The world survived only if people pleased the gods, and human sacrifice was the offering Tezcatlipoca desired most.

The high priest rose from his jaguar-shaped throne. He chanted a prayer as he walked toward Yaolt. When the priest raised his flint knife, Yaolt lifted his head, straining to watch. He wanted to see his own heart ripped from his chest and held pulsing to the sky before his spirit left his body and journeyed on.

The knife came down. Its tip pierced Yaolt's

skin, and blood spattered his forehead. He tensed, expecting an explosion of pain. But before the cutting edge sliced deeper, a thunderclap shook the pyramid. Lightning streaked across the sky and shadowy hands tore Yaolt from the priests.

At first, Yaolt thought Tezcatlipoca had come and taken him to the land of the dead. But he soon realized he had been kidnapped and imprisoned in another world. He hid his identity from his captors and veiled his secret knowledge with lies, fearful the ancient prophecies had come true.

CHAPTER ONE

BERTO GLANCED at his watch again, anxious for everyone to leave. An hour had passed since Quake had closed, and couples still lingered near the entrance, laughing and kissing as if they didn't want the party to end but didn't know where else to go. The true clubbers had already left for Hex, an illegal after-hours club in the flower market downtown. Berto didn't understand the stragglers. Without the music and the crowd, the magic was gone, and Quake was once again no more than an empty building in an abandoned oil field.

"Berto, come to Hex with us." Tabitha and Ana startled him from his thoughts. They were regulars, but he hadn't seen the girl with them at the club before.

"I can't," Berto said. Normally he just worked the ropes, deciding who went inside and who waited in line. He usually left as soon as the club closed, but since L.A. nights had become more dangerous, his boss had asked him to stay until every last clubber left.

"You don't believe all that trash about aliens from outer space abducting kids for experiments, do you?" Ana asked and smoothed her hands down her sides in a slow tease.

"What else could it be?" the new girl answered before Berto could. "They found circles burned into the sidewalks near the cars and—"

"Courtney," Tabitha interrupted, and rolled her eyes. "If spaceships were flying overhead, don't you think we'd see them? At least, the air force would."

Courtney shrugged, but she didn't look convinced. Then she focused on Berto. "Come with us." She tilted her head in a pose that looked rehearsed.

"Sorry," he answered.

"We need a bodyguard." Ana arched her back and stretched her arms in a mock yawn. Her low-riding skirt slipped below her hip bones. "You don't want us walking down Fourth Street alone, do you?"

"I want you to be careful," Berto answered.

Even with its reputation for freakiness, Hex was probably safer than the deserted streets near Quake. The newspapers were giving front-page coverage to the kidnappings. Seventeen high-school students had disappeared so far. A radio-talk-show host connected the abductions to the coming solar eclipse, claiming cults were stealing kids for human sacrifice. But Berto feared something worse, and tonight he sensed it more strongly.

"It's cold," Ana said in a peevish tone, and folded her arms over her chest. "Where's my car?"

"I'll check." Berto walked back to Eli, the only valet still on duty. He was helping the last couple into a silver Altima.

Now, besides the three girls, only one guy remained. He stood slouched against the fence, wearing sunglasses and a rhinestone-studded jacket, his white hair moussed into spikes. Berto hadn't let him into the club and sometimes the rejects waited until Berto was alone to find out why they hadn't made the cut. Berto sighed. He'd have to think of a lie to make the guy feel good about himself and want to come back. He didn't want to say anything that could discourage the kids who waited in line every night. But more than that, Berto didn't want to depress the guy with the truth.

"Why haven't you brought Ana's car around?" Berto asked Eli.

"Man, haven't you caught on yet?" Eli said. "She hasn't even asked me. She's been stalling because she wants to hook up with you." Eli opened a cupboard and pulled out a set of keys connected to a silver heart inscribed with the word *heartbreaker*. "Why don't you just go out with her?"

"I'm a game to her," Berto answered. "Ana and Tabitha have a bet going to see which one of them will date me first."

"I wish they'd bet on me." Eli grinned and

ran off, his tennis shoes slapping against the sidewalk.

Berto leaned against the building and watched the girls standing at the curb. Eli didn't understand. The girls didn't want to spend time alone with Berto; they wanted the conquest—"bragging rights," he had overheard Ana say.

Tabitha and Ana opened their purses and pulled out small notebooks. Ana scribbled something, then showed Courtney and Tabitha the page. Tabitha squealed in approval and swayed her hips in a dance.

"How can you write that?" Courtney asked.

"You'll get used to grading guys." Tabitha smirked and glanced knowingly at Berto. "There's only one who rates an A."

"What if Sledge reads what you've written about him?" Courtney asked Ana.

"Who cares? It's the truth. He kisses like my cocker spaniel." Ana snapped the notebook closed and dropped it into the pink purse dangling from a strap around her shoulder. "It's better if he finds out, so he can change. Then his girlfriend won't have to suffer."

"You kissed him knowing he has a girl-friend?" Courtney looked surprised.

"You're too goody-goody," Tabitha said. "Don't be afraid of hurting someone's feelings. It's not like a guy wouldn't do that to you. They're all alike. Isn't that right, Berto?"

"No," Berto answered.

"We know better," Ana challenged, turning away from him.

Berto started to defend himself, but before he could speak, a sudden light blinded him. His arm shot up to shield his face. The glare died suddenly, leaving a blizzard of white spots in his vision. His eyes felt dry and gritty with sunburn. He blinked the afterimages away but saw nothing around him that could have explained the flash.

Then Eli parked Ana's Land Rover at the curb and jumped out. The headlights were on. Maybe the beams had streaked over Berto at an odd angle and caused the burst of brightness. Apparently he was the only one who had seen it. The girls didn't seem disturbed. Courtney and Tabitha crowded together, checking their makeup in the side-view mirror.

"Hurry," Ana said, and handed Eli five dollars before she crawled in behind the steering wheel.

Tabitha started to get into the back, then glanced over her shoulder and stopped. "We're the last ones, Berto. You can go with us now."

"I can't leave yet." Berto started to point to the guy at the fence, but the sidewalk behind him was empty. He cursed under his breath. The newspapers had reported the kidnappings happening that way: the person there, then gone. He should never have let the girls absorb his attention the way he had. He headed over to the fence to investigate, expecting to find burn marks in the concrete.

"Berto."

Someone tugged at his jacket. He turned, and Courtney bumped into him. She started to fall, but he caught her and held her in his arms, her warmth chasing away the night cold. Her long hair spilled over his hands, and she looked up at him with an inviting gaze. He released her, but she didn't step away.

"Ana said we could give you a ride," Courtney offered breathlessly, her fingers gliding over his belt buckle. "Please come with us."

Berto felt ambushed. Tabitha and Ana had set him up, knowing he wouldn't want to hurt Courtney's feelings.

"I'll make it fun," Courtney persisted. She was obviously crushing on him, but her attraction had nothing to do with who he was. Girls who identified too strongly with being nice became infatuated with bad boys in order to feel whole; they needed someone to express their darker, unacceptable side, the part they kept hidden, even from themselves. Berto looked the part: a motorcycle-riding guy dressed in black, with a mysterious, troubled look and a bad-ass reputation.

Courtney misinterpreted Berto's silence for a go-ahead and started to wrap her arms around his waist.

He caught her wrists before she could hug him, his fingers instinctively searching for her pulse. The rapid beat of her heart stirred an intense need inside him. He let go, hoping it wasn't too late.

"Are you afraid to kiss me?" she teased.

Berto clenched his teeth until his jaws ached, fighting the desire to pull her back and place his lips on hers. He wished he could tell her the real reason he couldn't hold her. But even if he did, she wouldn't believe him.

"You don't have anything to fear from me," she went on, and let her fingers run over the top of her silky halter, imitating one of Ana's moves. He wondered if she practiced in front of a mirror.

"Don't act this way, Courtney," he said and looked away. Something in the dark had caught his attention. Had he only imagined the movement?

"Act like what?" She touched his cheek, pulling him back toward her until his eyes met hers again.

"You're too eager," he answered. "Guys take advantage of that."

"You didn't," she argued flirtatiously, and leaned against him.

"I would have taken advantage of you—"

He caught himself. He had almost said, *if I were an ordinary guy*. He started to speak again, but a sliver of black streaked across the shadows, and this time he felt certain he hadn't imagined it. A dark cloud billowed against the stucco wall. He realized his mistake—his attraction to Courtney had made him forget the danger. He took her arm and guided her back toward the car. Tabitha and Ana were watching him intently from inside.

"You're too willing to please," he said to Courtney.

"I don't try to—" She stopped. "You think it's wrong to be nice?"

"When you get home tonight," he said, quickening their pace, "look in the mirror and ask yourself how you would act if you made yourself the center of your life."

"Be selfish?" She looked stunned.

"Stop trying to please guys. Put yourself first. If you don't change, some guy is going to break your heart. I promise." But that was the least of his worries right now. He felt unfriendly eyes watching him.

"Tabitha and Ana—" she began defensively.

"They only please themselves," he said, feeling vulnerable and exposed. What was stalking him?

"They please guys," Courtney said, blushing.

"Ana and Tabitha are players," he answered. "You're not."

"Are you saying I'm a prude?" She pulled away from him.

A shift in the darkness made him turn and look back, but what had been there, if anything had, was gone. Maybe the movement had been only a trick of clouds and reflected city lights, but still his stomach tightened nervously, and he sensed that something in the night had changed. He wanted nothing more than to see the three girls safely on their way to Hex.

"You need to go," he said abruptly, and hurried her to the car. Her spiked sandals tapped rapidly on the concrete.

When he opened the car door, she threw herself into the front seat and looked back at him with a mixture of shock and distress, her eyes reddening with tears.

"What did he say to you?" Ana asked.

Berto closed the door and lingered by the window, watching Courtney.

"He said he was afraid I'd take advantage of him and break his heart," Courtney lied. Her scowl dared Berto to contradict her.

Ana and Tabitha squealed, as if they had scored a winning point.

"We're going to have you, Berto," Ana yelled from the window. "That's a promise. Someday."

Tires shrieked, and smoke from burning rubber made Berto cough. The car sped away, music from the stereo blasting into the night. Tabitha stuck her bare leg out the window and started rolling a black fishnet stocking over her toes, getting ready for Hex.

"Man, how can you say no to a carload of girls like those?" Eli asked. "You must be either dumb or in love."

"I guess I'm both," Berto answered, but his mind was on his growing sense of unease.

He nudged Eli and they began walking around the building to the employees' parking lot.

"Did you see that guy at the fence leave?" Berto asked.

"You mean Pete?" Eli didn't wait for an answer. "He's probably chasing Ana and Tabitha over to Hex right now." Eli took a neat roll of bills from his pocket and started counting them. "I see him waiting for them every night."

But Berto didn't think Pete had snuck away to follow the girls. He glanced back at the fence, convinced now that the explosion of light was somehow related to Pete's abrupt disappearance. Maybe aliens had taken him, beamed him up in a flash.

By the time they reached Eli's rusted Pontiac, Berto sensed a change in the atmosphere. The air felt heavy, the way it does before a violent storm. That meant only one thing to Berto; something from another world was breaking through into this one.

"Let me give you a ride to your bike," Eli said as he climbed into the Pontiac and turned the key in the ignition. The engine knocked, rocking the car, and the sudden sound startled Berto. Only then did he realize how nervous he had become.

"I'll be all right," Berto answered.

"See you tomorrow, then." Eli drove off, and Berto jogged across the asphalt, his mind set on returning to the sidewalk where Pete had been standing.

He didn't notice the electrical hum of the security lights until the sound rose to a shrill pitch. Lights blazed, and then, one by one, shattered, spraying glass across the parking lot. Red sparks showered over him, and he was left alone in the shadow of the building.

He told himself a circuit had failed, but he knew that was a lie. He had been so worried about the safety of others that he hadn't thought about his own, and, of all the people in the club, he was the one with the most to fear, because he and his roommates were Renegades, fugitives from Nefandus, a world paralleling this one, where he had been enslaved.

He rubbed his jacket sleeve, feeling the

scars beneath the fabric. A branding iron had given him the scars, marking him as a *servus*. His roommates each had one disfiguring welt burned into the skin. He had two.

From the corner of his eye, he glimpsed a figure darting across a nearby field. But when he turned to look where the phantom had been, he saw only the distant oil pumps. In the dim light the machines looked like donkeys' heads, nodding up and down, their constant movement filling the night with mechanical clanging.

He strained to hear the other quiet sounds that meant someone from the other side was passing through. Usually a portal was needed to journey from one world to the next, but some bounty hunters could shift between dimensions from any location. Maybe one was stalking him now, hoping to capture him and take him back to Nefandus for a reward.

But being hunted by a *venator* wasn't his greatest fear. Regulators sometimes came into this world, and they were far more treacherous. They policed Nefandus and served the ancient evil that ruled there.

Slow, stealthy footsteps crunched over the broken glass.

"Who's there?" Berto asked, his heart thudding violently. As soon as the words left his mouth he felt foolish. Did he really expect the person hiding from him to answer?

He waited, holding his breath, and listened, but silence now claimed the dark.

A breeze slithered around him, bringing the ocean damp, and stirring dead weeds with a soft rustling. He fought back his fear. Reason told him that Regulators and bounty hunters wouldn't play this cat-and-mouse game with him. If someone was hiding, waiting to jump him, it had to be a person from this world, someone with reason to exercise caution.

Maybe Pete had been more upset about being rejected than Berto had assumed. This wouldn't be the first time a wannabe clubgoer had tried to take out his anger on Berto.

Then, in his peripheral vision, Berto caught furtive movement. Whoever was stalking him was clever, but Berto had skills of his own. While imprisoned in Nefandus, his master had given him the ability to transform. He could dematerialize into shadow and float across the sky. Shape-shifting had been as normal there as driving a car was here, and Berto hadn't lost the knack. He shook his arms and concentrated on releasing his body. He grinned, imagining the surprise on the face of his attacker when he lunged at Berto and fell through black mist.

Berto was close to the corner of the building. In a few more steps he'd be back under the comforting glow of a street lamp, but when he started forward, blackness thickened on the stucco wall, tightening into a huge silhouette.

Maybe he had been wrong after all, and a bounty hunter was materializing. He paused and stared at the blotch forming. The cloud continued to pull together until it became a person standing in the emergency exit doorway.

Instinct told Berto to run, but instead he went back the way he had come, staying close to the building. He needed to know who was stalking him and why.

The figure lumbered toward him.

Berto paused, and when he did, the world

seemed to tilt. A strange heaviness bore down on him, giving him the feeling that he was walking deep below the surface of a lake. He blinked against the dizziness that made the night spin and desperately tried to find his balance. He stumbled and hit the wall, biting his lip. The taste of blood flooded his mouth.

His sense of danger grew, and he struggled to turn, scraping his hands on the rough stucco. He tried to pull himself around the corner into the safety of the street, but thick, gluey air encircled him. A chill penetrated to his bones, and his legs became sluggish as his body went numb.

That was the last he remembered until a cramp in his foot made him open his eyes. A sticky sweetness filled his mouth. Dew speckled his jacket, and desert sage scented the air. How long had he been standing there?

Maybe he had been abducted by space aliens and returned after the extraterrestrials had finished their experiments on him. He felt something cold on his chest and glanced down, expecting to see black rings encircling his feet, but what he saw startled him more.

CHAPTER TWO

A GIRL STOOD next to Berto, her hands under his shirt. Her fingertips prodded his bare chest in a way that made him think she was hunting for his heartbeat. He tried to move, but his body felt sedated, his feet unresponsive, and then he became aware of an eerie stillness.

"What's wrong?" he asked.

She let out a startled cry, as if his voice had frightened her. She glanced up, her eyes widening, and when she saw him watching her, she spun away, ripping his shirt. Buttons flew and pinged across the asphalt. She hid her face in her hands.

"Did you escape?" Berto asked, assuming

that she had. The sweet scent from the magic fires in Nefandus still clung to her. She wore the familiar tunic of a *serva*, but her green high-top sneakers baffled him; slaves weren't normally allowed such shoes.

She shook her head and backed away from him.

"Don't be afraid of me," he said gently.

New Renegades were usually shocked to find themselves in Los Angeles, and the girl definitely looked dazed.

"I can help you," he offered, shaking the numbness from his arms and legs.

She peeked out at him through her spread fingers and mumbled something.

"I can't understand you," he said, trying to pull her hands away from her mouth, but when he touched her, she dematerialized in a burst. Her silhouette hovered above him, then spread into a vapor that blew about, ruffling his hair. At last her shadow self spiraled up and disappeared with an angry shriek.

Abruptly the world came alive again. Wind gusted around him, flapping his torn shirt about and breaking the odd quiet. Cars whirred down Sepulveda Boulevard on the other side of the grade, and the mechanical pumps made hard metallic clanks. He looked around, wondering what had caused the temporary stillness, but then he remembered Pete and charged forward, determined to investigate.

Near the fence where Pete had stood, a circle was scorched into the sidewalk. Berto wiped his hand over the blackened concrete. Fine ash coated his palm. He stared at the soot, and an idea came to him. Maybe he knew what had caused the disappearances of Pete and the seventeen other high-school students.

He ran across the street to the vacant lot, straddled his motorcycle, and raced away, eager to return to the loft apartment and share his theory with his roommates. At the corner, he pushed hard on the right grip to make the turn. The engine's roar vibrated through him as he buzzed down Sepulveda.

By the time he crossed the railroad tracks near See's candy store, his mind had wandered back to the girl. He hoped she was all right.

Thinking about her reminded him of the day he had arrived in L.A.

Like all Renegades, he had assumed that he would return to his home. Instead he had found himself trapped three thousand years away. His roommates admired the way he had adjusted to the twenty-first century, but Berto longed to go back to his own time and take his place in the Toltec Nation.

Even now it was hard for him to believe the changes in his life. He and his roommates were the Four of Legend, destined to destroy Nefandus and free its *servi*. Berto had always imagined that the Four would be avenging angels with fiery halos and raven wings, supernatural creatures strong enough to fight Regulators and magic—not four guys who had trouble doing their homework and paying the rent.

More than anything, they needed a guide—someone to help them understand their powers. Each of Berto's roommates had a magical gift. Obie was a rune master, but his spell-casting often had unexpected consequences that took days to undo.

Kyle created things by imagining them. That ability might have been useful, except everything he generated quickly turned into foul-smelling slime.

Samuel could call forth power animals. Yet he couldn't send the creatures back. So, most often a coyote lived with them, and sometimes a bear. Berto hated the way the animal smell spread through the apartment, but at least they had finally gotten rid of the fleas.

The motorcycle sped past the Cathedral of Our Lady of the Angels, and moments later he turned left and zoomed under the dragon gateway into Chinatown. He parked near the metro overpass on Alameda Boulevard and glanced up. The lights were still shining in the top windows of the old mill. Then Berto heard the haunting tones of Obie's guitar.

Soon he was in the elevator, heading up to the fourth floor. He unlocked the back door and stepped into the kitchen.

The coyote stood on its hind legs in front of the sink, licking water from the dripping faucet. Berto started to scold the animal, but then he saw Obie's pet iguana bathing in the coyote's water bowl. The coyote whined and padded over to Berto, nails clicking on the concrete floor.

"Sorry, old guy," Berto said, and grabbed a pan from the cupboard. "I know you hate living inside." He rubbed the coyote behind the ears, then walked to the sink and stopped. A greenish gray slime clogged the drain. The stench was overpowering.

Kyle had obviously been practicing and had tried to grind up the remains in the garbage disposal. Berto touched the gluey stuff, mystified. How could Kyle create something from nothing?

Berto ran water into the pan and set it on the floor for the coyote, then turned back and studied the mess in the sink. Kyle had once said that the residue was ectoplasm, the same substance that came off mediums when they communicated with spirits, but it smelled more like decomposing fish.

The kitchen door banged open, jolting him from his thoughts. Samuel walked in, balancing four pizza boxes. He was bare-chested and didn't seem self-conscious about the thick scars on his back, from the whippings he had received in Nefandus. Like Berto, Samuel was from a different era. His home had been the eighteenth-century American frontier. He smiled when he saw Berto.

"You missed dinner," he said, holding up the grease-stained boxes. "Want some?"

Berto shook his head. "I don't know how you can eat in this stinking air."

"I was lost in the wilderness once and tried to eat skunk. So I guess after that I can eat anything," Samuel said, pushing a chunk of pepperoni into his mouth. He shoved the boxes into the refrigerator and joined Berto at the sink.

"Amazing, isn't it?" Samuel continued. "A little while ago, this sludge was the biggest man-killing monster I'd ever seen." He pointed to the broken ceiling fan, as if offering proof. "Kyle conjured a beast that looked like something one of the members of the Inner Circle could have made."

The Inner Circle was the assembly of rulers in Nefandus. They sometimes fought each other, but instead of throwing punches, they conjured beasts to do their fighting for them.

"I warned him not to go so fast," Berto said. "He isn't ready."

Berto left Samuel and hurried into the next room, determined to confront Kyle. Tension between them had been building since Kyle had decided that the real purpose of his gift was to create monsters capable of fighting off those summoned by the members of the Inner Circle.

Obie stopped playing his guitar when Berto entered the room. In his own time, Obie had been a Visigoth warrior who had fought in battles alongside his father, the Goth king Filimer. Now he played in a band called Pagan. Obie looked eager to talk to Berto, but Kyle remained at his easel, painting golden scales on a dragon.

"Sorry about the mess." Kyle spoke before Berto could. His tone didn't sound apologetic.

"The creature could have turned on you," Berto said.

"You're right," Kyle answered. "I won't do it again."

Kyle seemed unconcerned, and that worried Berto. Normally Kyle was the one who was serious-minded, verging on being high-strung, but since he had discovered who his father was, he had changed, and his new attitude annoyed Berto.

"Come look at this." Obie broke in, as if sensing a fight brewing. He pushed aside the tubes of oil paint scattered about Kyle's work table and spread out a map of L.A. "All the kidnappings took place along this line. I think the Inner Circle is planning to invade the earth realm soon and needs more *servi* to execute its plan."

"That's a possibility," Berto said, anxious to share his theory. "But what if the boundary between the two worlds is weakening? Maybe kids are falling through."

"Why would you think that?" Kyle set his paintbrush down and joined them.

"Someone disappeared outside Quake tonight," Berto explained. "And I'm sure I accidentally stumbled into the boundary." He told them everything that had happened, and when he finished, he added, "The girl was a *serva*, but I doubt she was trying to escape. I think she had unintentionally crossed over at the same time I fell into the border."

"But what about the burn marks?" Kyle asked. "How would you explain the charred circles?"

"That's what gave me the idea," Berto went on. "It was something Samuel said about nuclear fusion when he was helping me with my homework."

"Nuclear fusion?" Kyle repeated, a mixture of doubt and worry showing on his face.

"Berto's right," Samuel answered from the doorway to the kitchen. "When we go through the portal our atoms reconfigure to fit with those of Nefandus. So if the boundary is becoming unstable, then maybe a kind of nuclear fusion is taking place."

"But how?" Kyle didn't look convinced.

"When atoms like hydrogen combine and form heavier atoms, energy is released, usually as heat," Samuel said. "That could explain the scorch marks. When kids fall into the boundary, maybe hydrogen seeps in with them. After all, it is the most abundant element in our universe." Samuel loved science and surprised them all by excelling in it at school. "It's a possibility, anyway."

Obie nodded. "But maybe the boundary is being purposely weakened so that invading troops can come through without having to make a transition first."

"Is that possible?" Berto asked, looking at Samuel.

"Magic can do anything," Samuel answered with a shrug.

"I think we should go into Nefandus and check around," Kyle offered. His words hung in the air like a bad omen.

"We're not ready yet," Samuel answered and looked away, avoiding Kyle's gaze.

"Why not?" Kyle asked. "We know the risks. We've gone before."

"It's not like we could do anything," Obie said, folding the map. "Our powers aren't strong enough yet."

"What do you think?" Kyle stared at Berto, obviously impatient for his answer.

"Let's wait," Berto said, shielding the real reason he and the others didn't want Kyle to return to Nefandus, not yet anyway.

Kyle had been deeply in love with Catty, a goddess and Daughter of the Moon. Her destiny had been to face the Atrox, the ancient evil enthroned in Nefandus, but something had happened to make her turn to the dark. Now she lived with her father, a member of the Inner Circle, and rumors had spread that she was fulfilling an unholy prophecy, reversing the destiny for which she had been born.

Berto didn't think it would take much convincing for Kyle to switch sides and join Catty, especially now that he had learned that his own father was one of three demons created from the cosmic dust.

"Maybe it's time for us to fulfill the Legend," Kyle tried again. "We could sneak into Hawkwick's library. The books must contain the answers we need."

While the others argued, Berto stepped

back and studied his friends. They acted brave, but he knew they spent restless nights just as he did, wondering about their future. How could they fulfill the Legend? No one could go against the Atrox and defeat it. They definitely needed more information, and Kyle was right about one thing: the books in Hawkwick's library were supposed to have the answers. Berto weighed his options. It was too dangerous for Kyle to return to Nefandus right now, and Obie was still vulnerable to his old master's power. That left Samuel. But breaking into Hawkwick's library with Samuel was chancy, because the coyote could suddenly appear and give them away. Even though the risk was great, Berto decided to go there alone, without telling the others.

CHAPTER THREE

BERTO STEPPED into his bedroom and closed the door without turning on the lights. He brushed his hand over his bookcase, sorting through the clutter, until his fingers found a box of matches. Then he stepped reverently to an altar in the corner and struck a match. A flame hissed and the blaze was reflected in a shiny obsidian rock. He chanted softly as he lit three cones of incense.

Within the black volcanic glass something stirred. He blew out the match, but a fire continued to smolder in the stone, casting faint golden light about the room. Berto whispered his prayers so his voice couldn't be heard. His roommates had asked him to stop praying to Tezcatlipoca. They thought the lord of the smoking mirror was an evil deity, but Berto knew his god was a force of good.

He started another song, barely moving his lips. The fire grew brighter within the stone, and when it did, he saw something on his bed. He switched on his lamp, certain his eyes had deceived him. A broken clay flute lay on his tangled bedspread.

The shattered pottery triggered memories of his life long ago. For one year he had lived in luxury as the earthly incarnation of Tezcatlipoca. During the day he had remained hidden inside the temple studying, but at night he had dressed as the god, his arms and legs weighted with bangles of seashells that rattled noisily as he danced through the streets with his eight attendants. He had played his flute, and everyone who heard his music had believed the god himself was passing by their homes. Some brought out sick children for Berto's blessing, believing his touch could cure them.

He remembered the sweet taste of the

offerings given to him, the fragrance of the flowers thrown at him. A sob caught in his throat as his homesickness became unbearable. He touched the thin scar on his breastbone. He had told only Ashley of the death that had been denied him. She must have been the one who had left the broken flute, but why?

He picked up a shard and puzzled over it, turning it in his hands, searching for a message.

The words *too dangerous* had been etched into the fragment. Without bothering to read more, he scooped up the rest of the pieces and threw them aside. The ceramic was still hitting the wall as he closed his eyes and let stillness invade his mind.

Slowly his spirit left his body, a shimmering replica of himself. That was his gift. He was a dream walker, and, in his sleep, or in a trance, his soul could separate itself from him and travel to distant places.

The journey wasn't without risk; while his spirit roamed, his body remained open and unguarded, easy for demons and lost spirits to possess. He often wondered what would happen if he returned and found his body occupied by another entity.

But that wasn't the only danger. A silver cord connected his spirit to his body, and if someone severed it, he wouldn't be able to find his way back. Even with the dangers, he preferred to visit Ashley this way. If he turned to shadow, it would take too long to cross the city to her condo on the Santa Monica beach, and she was leery of shadows because she had made many enemies in Nefandus.

Berto stepped from his physical body, a ghost, able to pass through walls and remain invisible unless he chose to be seen. He floated up and soon found himself in a dense fog, with openings into several other dimensions. But he didn't travel to the spirit worlds or the heavenly spheres. He preferred to stay close to earth, on this cloudy astral plane.

In less than a minute, he glided down into moonlight, the soft lulling rhythm of the surf surrounding him. Then he saw Ashley. She stood on her balcony, staring at the night sky, her face illuminated by candle flames flickering in the tin lanterns along the railing. Astrological charts lay rolled out on the table behind her, the edges fluttering in the breeze. She rubbed her temples, as if something were troubling her.

Berto wondered if the coming solar eclipse was making her uneasy. She believed that the stars, moons and planets influenced human lives, and had told him that an eclipse was always a bad omen.

His spirit drifted closer and caressed her arm. She turned slowly, as if she had sensed a whisper of air. The sadness in her eyes made him long to hold her as he once had. They had been *servi* together, working in the dig, and together they had escaped. But she had been desperate to go home to ancient Mesopotamia and had betrayed her own kind by becoming a *venatrix*, a bounty hunter. The Inner Circle had granted her freedom to come and go between the two realms, and for every Renegade she returned, she was rewarded additional power to time-travel.

Berto bent closer and kissed her cheek. He didn't understand why she had left the broken flute. Maybe it had only been to taunt him. Reluctantly, he started to return to his body.

"Don't go," Ashley whispered, and her hand brushed through him. "I need to talk to you."

ASHLEY'S HAND reached out again, and Berto flitted back, unsure. The vibrations from her first touch still quivered through him. He started to leave, then hesitated. How could she know he was there? No one could see him unless he willed it.

"I'm talking to you, Berto," she said.

"Why didn't you tell me you could see me?" Berto asked in a thin, ghostly whisper. He felt humiliated.

"I didn't want to spoil my fun," she said, stepping closer to him. "I'm glad you're here tonight."

His mind raced back to other visits. How

many times had he told Ashley he couldn't stand her and then, that same day, astrally projected to look after and guard her? Had she always known he was watching her, even when she had kissed other Renegades and Followers—

"If you're going to spy on me," she said with a knowing smile, "then you can't be upset if you see me kissing someone else, can you?" She caught the silver cord, and a shudder raced through him. She whirled, wrapping it around her, and stopped inches from him, her breath making him waver.

"Don't be jealous," she said. "None of them meant anything to me."

He tried to pull away from her, but she had ensnared him. She played with the cord, teasing him and making him aware that she could break his link to life with one snap of her fingers.

"Why do we always waste time fighting with each other when what we really want is to be together?" she asked with a sad smile and kissed the tether. She ran it over her bottom lip, and he sighed.

"You're the one who makes it impossible,"

he started to argue, but then he stopped. "I don't know." He wanted to be with her, but past experience had taught him not to trust her. Carefully, he started disentangling himself from her hold.

"I need to talk to you," Ashley said, tugging on the cord and keeping him bound to her. "Hex is still open. Meet me there in an hour." Then, without waiting for his answer, she dissolved into luminous dust and disappeared into the night.

Her abrupt departure troubled Berto. Ashley lived near a portal used by Regulators, and this wouldn't be the first time she had betrayed him. His feelings for her had made him careless. He glanced about, expecting Regulators to form in the flickering shadows.

He willed his spirit back, and the astral plane flashed past him. He slammed into his body. Pain radiated through him as his soul readjusted to the confinement of flesh and bone. His heart loped, skipping a beat, before finally settling into its natural rhythm. He grabbed the edge of the bed, trying to steady himself, and blinked until his vision returned.

Low voices came from the other room. His roommates were still awake, but he was too embarrassed to tell them what had happened. He knew they would try to talk him out of meeting Ashley, or worse, insist on going with him, and he wanted time alone with her. He changed out of his torn shirt and put on a blue sweater, then grabbed his leather jacket, ran a hand through his hair, and started toward the door.

Reason told him to be cautious, but he recklessly turned to shadow and streaked under his door, then out into the cold night through a crack in the hallway window.

He materialized in an alley downtown and started walking. He knew better than to hope this meeting with Ashley meant more than it did, but his mind was already fast-forwarding, envisioning them together as a couple again.

Sudden barking made him stop. Then, from the apartments overhead, howls and yelps joined the first dog's warning cry. A shadow slid along the wall beside him, trilling in a high-pitched voice. The gauzy splotch paused, as if aware Berto was watching it, and then drew itself together.

Berto sensed it was the girl who had appeared to him earlier that evening.

"Stay with me this time," he said. "I can help you."

Her answer was as unintelligible as before, but she had a new somber tone that worried him.

"I can't understand you," Berto said softly, afraid of frightening her away. "Materialize and tell me. I promise I won't hurt you."

Her shadow churned nervously, eventually thickening behind a Dumpster. The toes of her green tennis shoes stuck out in the light.

"I'm trying to warn you," she said petulantly. "Don't you understand anything?"

A chill swept through him. "Tell me."

"I have been," she answered sharply.

Something moved in the air above them, and at first he thought that alley cats were jumping around on the fire escape. He didn't see anything on the iron stairs, but the atmosphere around them had definitely changed.

"Damn," the girl muttered, her voice tight with fear.

He sensed she was going to disappear again, and he needed to hear her warning. He lunged forward, determined to catch her and make her speak. He grabbed her shoulders. She shrieked, exploding into points of black that swept around him, striking his face like windblown sand, and then she vanished.

CHAPTER FIVE

VENDORS CROWDED the street in front of the flower market, carrying flowers and potted plants to and from trucks. Berto leaped over a line of white plastic buckets filled with carnations and almost bumped into two men unloading red roses from a van. When they turned, Berto stole a bouquet. A thorn pricked his thumb, and he licked the blood, then smiled to himself. According to ancient lore, if Ashley accepted the rose with his blood on it, she would love him for eternity.

He sprinted to a vacant coffee shop on the corner. The boarded-up door was a ploy to keep the unwelcome away. He pushed against the plywood, and the rusted hinges creaked open, allowing him entry. He slipped inside and walked along the dusty counter. A mirror, covering the length of one wall, shimmered with the vibration of the music in the next room, but the music itself couldn't be heard inside the abandoned café.

Where the entrance to the kitchen had once been, he pulled aside a heavy drape and opened a padded door. Immediately, hands grabbed him and pulled him into a narrow hallway. A newcomer might have been startled by the search, but Berto knew the routine. He raised his arms, trying to protect the roses, and let the three punkers pat him down. Hollywood Drunk Punks worked security and, in the muted red light, their tattoos, silver septum rings, and the plugs stretching their earlobes gave them a scary, otherworldly appearance. Church keys clanked from chains connected to their belts, legal but lethal weapons.

Berto handed over a twenty-dollar bill. Another door opened, and he was shoved into a surreal world. Music boomed around him, the air humid and warm. Strobe lights shuddered and made the crowd appear to jump repeatedly. He stepped into the throng as a guy with gold-capped teeth tried to sell him skittles. Berto shook his head and pushed on. Girls tried to pull him into the celebration but he continued working his way to the other side of the room where celebrities partied anonymously in the dark near a bank of windows. Velvet drapes barred the daylight and kept the night inside. A couple had wrapped themselves in the folds and were making out.

The music changed to a sultry song. Someone touched Berto's shoulder. He turned, expecting to see Ashley, and held the bouquet up offering her the roses.

But Courtney stood behind him, vamped out in a black bustier, her eyeliner curling into wings past the edges of her eyes. She grabbed the flowers before he could pull them away and buried her face in the petals.

"They said you wouldn't come to Hex," she said, obviously believing he was there to be with her.

"Who?" Berto asked, and followed her gaze.

Tabitha and Ana danced together, bodies slinking against each other, deliberately teasing the guys. They looked at Berto and grinned as if they thought Courtney's infatuation with him were a big joke. Berto's throat tightened in anger. He didn't want them using Courtney for their entertainment.

"They were wrong," Berto said and started dancing with Courtney. She wore a low-slung skirt, and he placed his palms flat on her bare hips, his thumbs stroking her tight stomach.

She took in a sharp breath and wrapped her arms around his neck. The rose petals tickled his ear.

"You told me to look in the mirror and ask myself how I would act if I made myself the center of my life," Courtney said. She pulled back and looked at him expectantly. "I decided I'd kiss you, whether you wanted me to or not."

She closed her eyes, parted her lips, and moved closer.

Berto put one finger on her mouth, her breath warm against his hand. Standing that close to her, feeling the softness of her skin, he was tempted to kiss her—but how many souls had he stolen already?

At times, he had tried to count, but he really didn't want to know. In Nefandus, his master had taken him into the earth realm and forced him to feed on the life force of others in order to keep his own spirit vigorous and strong.

The hunger was a curse put upon the *servi* to keep them enslaved. Even if they did escape, they would never find happiness in their freedom. They would be forced to live alone, or to destroy anyone they loved. One kiss was always the beginning; then the need took over.

A pleasant ache rushed through him, and the hunger became stronger than his will to hold it back. He cupped her sweet face in his hands and leaned down, imagining the taste of that first sip of her soul.

Courtney struggled, seeming to sense the danger in him now. The roses fell from her hand, and she pressed her palms against his chest. Her fear only sharpened his hunger. He tightened his hold and pressed his lips hard against hers. But instead of absorbing her life force, he spoke. "Don't let your friends stampede you into doing things you're not ready for. Promise me. Not everyone goes at the same pace."

He released her, but she didn't run.

She stepped back, her eyes glistening with tears, and stared at him. Clearly she was afraid of him, but mingled in with her fright he sensed an intense attraction to him.

He thought of his blood on the rose thorn.

"I'm sorry," he said, wishing he could free her from the spell. He had unintentionally condemned her to a horrible fate. He touched her shoulder to comfort her, and she flinched.

"Go," he said unpleasantly. "Your friends will think I kissed you, so you've won the bet."

She turned then and jostled through the dancers, heading for the exit.

Tabitha grabbed Courtney's arm and pulled her back. "You can't go without sharing," she yelled over the music.

"How was the kiss?" Ana asked, clearly jealous.

Courtney pressed her fingers against her

temples. "I want to go home," she said loudly. "I have a headache."

She used her elbows to make a path through the throng. Tabitha and Ana followed her, talking excitedly to each other.

Berto didn't need to be a mind reader to know that they assumed Courtney was leaving because Berto had done more than kiss her. He knew they were eager to hear the details so they could spread the gossip around Turney High.

"Why didn't you take her?" Ashley asked, surprising him. He hadn't been aware that she was standing nearby.

"Wouldn't you have been jealous if I had?" He touched her hair, brushing it back over her shoulder.

"Kissing an earthling is like getting a fresh drink of water." Ashley had also been trained to feed on souls, but she didn't try to control the darkness inside her.

She wrapped her hands around his neck and pulled him deeper into the crowd on the dance floor. Her body found the beat, and she moved seductively against him.

"I've missed you," she said over the music, her lips warm against his cheek.

He wanted to believe her, but could he trust her? He doubted she would bring Regulators there. Then again, Ashley never did what was expected. That was why she had become so successful as a bounty hunter.

"Haven't you missed me?" she asked. Her fingers played over the nape of his neck; then, gently, she pulled his head down until his mouth met hers. Ashley couldn't be harmed by his kiss as other girls could, because she had been a *serva*.

At last he gave in to his desire.

"It's too noisy in here," she said abruptly, pulling back before he was ready to end their kiss. "Let's go outside and talk."

For the second time that night he recklessly agreed, and moments later they were inside the flower market, strolling over the wet ground, a fanfare of potted plants and flowers surrounding them with a dizzying array of fragrances. The warehouse lights glared brightly. Berto picked up a fallen daisy and placed it in Ashley's hair.

She held his wrist and smiled up at him. "I need to ask a favor."

"I figured," he answered and tried to hide his disappointment.

"I want you to go into Nefandus and get a book for me," she said.

"You don't need me for that," he answered, hating the suspicion rising inside him. "You can buy the book easier than I can."

"The book isn't for sale," she said. "You'll need to steal it from Master Hawkwick's library."

He stared at her, trying to comprehend what she was asking. She couldn't know he had been planning to go there on his own. Then a miserable heaviness settled over him. She knew the danger, but evidently she didn't care. Did he mean so little to her? But he already knew the answer; he always had. She would do anything, no matter how terrible, if it furthered her chances of going home.

"Hawkwick won't be there," she said. "I've made sure of that."

"Ask Obie," Berto said angrily. "He was Hawkwick's *servus*. I wouldn't even know where to look." He strode away from her, feeling foolish, and dodged into the stairwell of the parking structure, determined to turn to shadow and leave.

She ran after him. "Don't go," she pleaded. "You haven't even let me finish, and already you're acting as if I'm sending you to your death."

The words hung in the air with prophetic resonance.

Ashley broke the stillness with a snicker. "You're immortal, after all. You can't die."

He looked away, not bothering to hide his annoyance.

"I need the book," she said quietly and, for a moment, he thought she was going to cry, but no tears came to her eyes.

"Then borrow it, Ashley," he said with rising frustration. He faded into an outline of himself. A sudden draft caught him and whisked him up the stairwell.

"I regret what I've done," she called after him. "I don't want to be a bounty hunter anymore."

He hovered, indecisive.

"What will happen to me if I tell *them* I'm done?" she asked. "I need the book so I'll know how to protect myself."

He materialized on the landing two flights above her and looked down over the railing. "Why can't you just stop?"

She huffed dismissively. "The members of the Inner Circle will never let me go. They've relied on me too often."

He walked down to her, his footsteps echoing behind him. "You're sure Hawkwick will be gone?"

"Positive."

He nodded. "I'll get the book."

But his answer didn't seem to please her. She appeared distressed.

"It's too dangerous," she said at last and started to leave. "I'll find another way. I don't know what I'd do if something happened to you."

"I'll be careful," he said, wondering why she seemed so reluctant now. "The portal opens tomorrow. I'll enter Nefandus then, but I need directions to Hawkwick's house."

She turned back and met his gaze, then slowly pulled a piece of notebook paper from her skirt pocket and unfolded it. "The title of the book is printed on one side. I drew a map to Hawkwick's apartment on the other."

Berto read the title and looked up. "*The History of Mesopotamia*? How is that going to protect you?"

"The answers are there," she answered firmly, her mood glum. "When you have the book, bring it to Olvera Street. I'll be waiting for you there."

Berto nodded, but his mind was already working on his own plan. He'd steal the book for Ashley, but while he was in Hawkwick's library, he planned to scout around and get some answers to a few questions of his own.

CHAPTER SIX

THE NEXT DAY, Berto walked down the breezeway at Turney High, toward the quad. The lunch period had started, but no one seemed to be leaving campus. Students were restless, and they had gathered in small groups, talking about the coming solar eclipse. Berto even overheard some of them making wild speculations about satanic cults or alien invasions.

Like everything that happened in L.A., someone had already figured out a way to make money from the recent scares. Most kids had purchased protective charms and crystals from street vendors, and they wore these around their necks. Many had on T-shirts featuring the picture of the eclipsed sun with a caption beneath that read: HAVE YOU BEEN ABDUCTED YET?

Berto found Samuel sitting at a picnic table with Maddie and her best friend, Emily. Samuel was eating a sandwich he'd made from pepperoni and cheese picked off someone's leftover pizza.

Berto handed him a breath mint. "You have got to find a job," he teased.

Maddie scowled at him.

"What's up?" Berto asked, surprised by her ice-cold reception.

"I can't believe you don't know," Maddie answered. Dark circles were visible beneath her usually vibrant eyes.

"So, tell him," Samuel said, and popped the last bite of sandwich into his mouth.

"Another guy from Turney is missing," she said, in an accusatory voice. "He went to Quake last night and never came home. His mother tried to call him on his cell phone, but all she got was a recording that said he had traveled out of area."

Berto knew she was talking about Pete, but he didn't let on.

"His car was found parked on a side street near the club," Emily added.

"Where were you?" Maddie demanded. "I thought it was your responsibility to—"

"Pete wasn't the only one abducted," Samuel interrupted, gently resting his hand on Maddie's.

"Seven more kids are missing," Emily put in. "Everyone thinks the abductions are related to the solar eclipse, like some cult is involved. My parents won't even let me go out after dark now. . . . Not that I care." She seemed to shudder, as if from a sudden chill, in spite of the warm sunshine.

"I know it's going to turn out to be something even worse than some crazy group with bizarre ideas about satanic rites," Maddie said, and her gaze settled on Berto.

Emily snapped the lid closed on her plastic lunch container. "Whoever it is, I wish the police would catch them soon. I'm scared to sleep alone in my own bedroom."

"It's not something the police are trained to handle," Maddie said with authority.

"Then why aren't you afraid?" Berto asked.

"Maybe you should be the one concerned," Maddie shot back.

"Why should he be?" Samuel asked, becoming defensive on behalf of Berto.

"Because I'm finally going to have the opportunity to prove that there's more to the universe than what we perceive with our five senses," she answered.

Berto stared at her blankly. Her tone implied a threat—but what did he have to fear from her?

"You make it sound like Berto is responsible," Samuel said. "Why would you even think that?"

Maddie stood suddenly, crumpling her lunch bag. "Because . . ." She looked from Berto to Samuel, and back to Berto again.

"Maddie?" Samuel tried to take her hand, but she turned and walked away.

But near the cafeteria Maddie turned back. "Emily, we're going to be late."

"For what?" Emily asked.

"Lunchtime Pilates," Maddie yelled and continued her march.

"Jeez, what's with her?" Emily stood and gathered her plastic containers. "Vampires were bad enough. But since the abductions started, she's been talking about people slipping into a parallel universe. I hope she doesn't expect me to go searching for another dimension with her. Not right now, anyway."

Berto exchanged quick glances with Samuel as Emily ran off to join Maddie.

"Why did you tell Maddie about Nefandus?" Berto asked.

"I didn't say anything to her," Samuel answered defensively. "You know I wouldn't."

"Then how did she come up with the idea about two worlds paralleling each other?" Berto questioned.

"By watching old movies and TV shows," Samuel said. "She believes in that kind of stuff, but it's more likely that Obie's spell is slipping."

"We don't need that now," Berto said

glumly, but he sensed Samuel was right; Obie's spell-binding wasn't as strong as it needed to be to hold Maddie's memories back indefinitely.

Maddie had witnessed Regulators kidnapping Kyle, Obie, and Berto. But instead of hiding, she had followed them to investigate, and a Regulator had captured her as well and taken her to Nefandus. Samuel had helped them all escape, and afterward Obie had cast a spell on Maddie to make her forget Nefandus.

"It's possible that she's starting to recall what really happened," Samuel went on. "She'd have more memories of time spent with you than the time she spent with the rest of us."

Berto nodded. Once Maddie had found them inside Nefandus, Berto had told her everything he could about that other world, hoping to ease her terror.

"I'll talk to Obie," Samuel said. "I'm sure he can fix the spell, but right now we have a bigger problem than Maddie getting her memories back."

"You're right," Berto agreed, but he couldn't stay and talk. He had less than an hour to get to the portal before it opened. He jumped up. "I'm going to cut my afternoon classes. I'll catch you later."

"Wait," Samuel called after him.

Berto pretended that he hadn't heard his friend. He charged across the quad, then ran down a deserted corridor to a janitor's closet and stole inside. Ammonia fumes stung his eyes as he let his body dissolve.

He started to drift under the crack at the bottom of the door, but drew back, surprised. Two pairs of sandaled feet waited on the other side. With a start he recognized Emily's hemp-and-seashell anklets and Maddie's purple toenails and silver toe rings. He elongated into a thread of shadow and slithered along a crack in the concrete until he was outside; then he blended into the shade of a palm tree and watched the two girls.

"Open the door," Maddie whispered anxiously.

"Why?" Emily asked, not moving.

"Because I want you to see." Maddie flung the door open. It hit the wall with a bang, and a mop fell over. She switched on the overhead light.

Emily looked into the storeroom, filled with brooms, dirty rags, and tubs of cleaning solution. "What did you think we'd find?"

Maddie ignored Emily's question and stepped inside. She studied the corners, as if she had expected Berto to jump out at her. "I know he came in here."

"Who?" Emily asked.

Maddie turned abruptly, grabbed Emily's wrist, and strode away, her sandals slapping against her heels. "Come on."

"Where to now?" Emily asked, running to keep up with Maddie's fast pace.

Berto didn't have time to wait and find out what they were up to. He let his shadow catch the wind and rode with it up over the school yard and across the freeway.

Moments later, he spiraled down and materialized in the old Chinatown plaza beneath a tree. Dusty red lanterns hung from the branches and swayed in the warm breeze.

A group of German tourists stood in front

of him, taking pictures of the pagoda-style buildings. When he was certain no one had seen him materialize, he walked up the incline to the fortune-teller's shop. Potted plants sat in front of the window, the leaves dripping water.

Berto pulled out a pocket watch and snapped it open. Instead of numbers, the face showed the changing position of stars and planets. He turned the dial, searching for the constellation of Perseus, and studied the stars forming Algol, the eye of Medusa. Hawkwick had taught Obie how to shift between dimensions from any location, but most Renegades, like Berto, had to wait until the demon star dimmed, signaling that the portal between the two worlds had opened. The ancients had believed that the eye blinked, but Algol was actually two stars revolving around each other in an eclipsing binary.

Minutes passed, and the demon star began to fade. The portal was opening. Berto glanced both ways. The walkway in front of the souvenir shops was empty. He stepped forward, his heart racing in anticipation of the dangers he was going to face in Nefandus. His nose touched the window.

"Berto, what are you doing?" Maddie and Emily ran up to him, carrying steaming buns from the bakery.

"It looked like you were going to walk right into the glass," Emily said excitedly, as if they had saved him.

Maddie had a more guarded, suspicious look.

"I thought you had a Pilates class," Berto said, positive they had been trailing him. But how would they have known to come here? They couldn't have followed his shadow across the freeway and over eight city blocks.

"Maddie made me ditch," Emily explained. "Can you imagine the trouble I'm going to be in? Her mother won't care, but my parents are strict."

"Samuel took me to the bakery," Maddie said. "And I wanted Emily to try the steamed milk buns. The red bean paste filling is incredible. Do you want a bite?" Maddie held up the roll, but her eyes remained focused on the window behind Berto.

"No, thanks," Berto answered. He glanced down at his watch, his anxiety rising. Soon, the portal would be closed.

"Why do you have two watches?" Maddie asked, and started to grab the one in his hand.

Berto snapped it shut and dropped it into his pocket.

"So, you never told us what you were doing here," Maddie said.

Berto couldn't come up with a plausible excuse. But then he saw someone inside the fortune-teller's shop. An old man was sitting at a table pouring a cup of tea. "I was going to have my fortune read," Berto lied.

He grabbed Emily and Maddie by the arms and escorted them into the small room. Diagrams of faces lined the walls, and the fragrance of freshly brewed jasmine tea wafted around them.

"But since you're here," Berto went on, "I'll let the two of you go first."

He eased Maddie into a metal folding chair

across from the old man. The legs scraped noisily over the concrete floor as Maddie struggled to stand up again. Berto pressed Emily down onto a wooden stool, and then he stepped back, ready to slip through the portal.

Maddie swung around. "I don't have any money," she said and started to leave.

Berto pulled out his wallet and blocked her way. He fumbled for a ten-dollar bill, got it out, and slapped it on the table.

"She needs her fortune read," he said.

The old man grinned and seemed eager to help Berto. "She has a big future ahead of her," the fortune-teller said. "One she would never have foreseen."

"That's what they all say," Maddie answered. She started to bolt, but the man cagily handed her his cup. Tea sloshed over the rim as Maddie held the bowl-like cup in her hands. For once, she seemed unsure.

"This will be fun," Emily said encouragingly. "I don't know why you're fighting it. You like this kind of thing."

The man gently clasped Maddie's chin in

his wrinkled hand, forcing her to look at him. He wore jade rings on his index fingers, and his nails were polished and cut short. "The deep gray color under your eyes tells me you have visitors at night," he said, in a concerned voice.

"You see that?" she asked in a faint whisper.

"The visitors mean you no harm," he answered. "You should listen to what they are telling you."

Berto stole outside the shop, then rushed back toward the storefront window, knocking over a potted plant. The glass vibrated against him, and for a moment he feared he was going to be forced to stay, but then the window melted around him, letting him enter.

Behind him, Emily screamed, and he knew she had witnessed him step through the glass and disappear. How was he going to explain that when he got back?

If he got back. A deeper voice mocked him. He sensed he would never return.

CHAPTER SEVEN

NUMBNESS HAD taken hold, and even though Berto knew what to expect when passing into Nefandus, the inability to move always panicked him; his heart grew still, his lungs stopped. His saliva thickened, and a cloyingly sweet taste gathered around his tongue. He needed to spit, but he could no longer work his mouth.

In the beginning, he had believed that Nefandus and earth existed side by side, but now he understood that the two realms were interlocked. The universe was composed of atoms, and within those atoms were spaces in which other atoms spun about, creating additional worlds. Scientists speculated that five or six dimensions existed simultaneously, each overlapping the other, their systems interwoven. Sometimes Berto wondered who lived in those other realms, but mostly he worried about what would happen when scientists discovered Nefandus.

Without warning, a dull ache rushed through him, and he braced himself for the fall. He plummeted from the portal, and before he could steady himself, he stumbled over a pile of dirt and bumped into a wheelbarrow piled high with bricks.

A flurry of stone chips struck him, stinging his face. One fragment cut his chin. He dove to the side of a small porch and peered out from behind the splintered steps, not understanding the sharp clanging and excited voices he was hearing.

Servi struck the cobblestones with pickaxes, shovels, and sledgehammers. Others stood in trenches, scooping dirt from ditches. Still others scaled the back of an apartment building, working chisels into the mortar and carelessly throwing bricks to the ground below. Even the gargoyles seemed to labor on the demolition, their granite claws prying at tiles and letting them slide off the roof.

Followers dodged the debris and yelled instruction to their *servi*. They appeared intent on wrecking the alley.

Berto had never seen such chaos in the city before. He glanced at the corner where the alley and road crossed each other, wondering if by some slip of atoms the portal had changed location, but the street signs still read DEVIL'S PALM and ELK HORN.

At last he stood and joined two *servi* marching behind a Follower who was holding a dousing rod. Too much pomade pasted the Follower's gray hair to his head. The man stopped as the stick bent in the direction of an untouched patch of cobblestones.

"Quickly, quickly, dig here," he ordered, raking his fingers over his scalp. When his hand fell back to his side, strands of hair remained rigidly on end, pointing toward the sky.

The taller of the two *servi* swung his

pickax. The chisel edge hit with a loud clang, and stone fragments pelted Berto.

"Why are they destroying the alley?" Berto asked, keeping his head bowed in the manner of the *servi*.

"They're searching for the black diamond," the *servus* answered.

Berto understood the wild excitement. Whoever possessed the wish-granting gem would have unlimited power. But Berto felt certain the diamond had hidden itself in the earth realm.

"Why do they think it's here?" Berto asked.

"The Oracle," the guy mumbled as he swung again.

"The master considers her a prophet and reads her newspaper column every day," the second one put in.

"She said the black diamond had concealed itself at the intersection of Elk Horn and Devil's Palm." The tall one smiled cunningly and wiped his forehead. The blisters on his hand were bleeding, but he didn't seem to mind. "The master has forgotten to give us the hana berry juice and—"

"We're going to run," the other interrupted in a low, excited voice. "Next time he turns his back we're going to try our luck and flee."

"Be careful," Berto whispered.

Regulators patrolled the alleyway, tromping back and forth. He sensed they had been sent to seize the diamond if anyone found it.

The first time Berto had encountered a Regulator he had thought the man was an inhabitant of Tlalocan, the dank and rotting underworld. Berto had never become used to their semblance to monsters or the stench of their decaying bodies. He still didn't understand what made Followers volunteer to serve the powerful entity that ruled Nefandus. Its evil infected those who gathered near it and slowly changed them into hideous imitations of what they had once been.

Berto snuck forward, keeping out of the way. He assumed the Regulators wouldn't notice him with everything else going on in the alley, but even if they did, he hoped his clothes and demeanor would make them believe he was one of the newly abducted *servi*. New arrivals were often found lost and terrified in this part of town.

The residents here had poor conjuring skills or none. It was easier for them to kidnap earthlings to do their work than to study and learn the science of magic. Most of them paid to have immortality and the power of transmutation given to their slaves, but some residents were even too impoverished to afford the mandatory hana berry juice all *servi* were supposed to drink. Berto pitied the ones who had to face Nefandus without the anesthetizing beverage.

He pulled out the notepaper Ashley had given him, but as he studied the map, he had a growing sense that someone was watching him. He looked up and caught the gaze of a Regulator. A shudder raced through Berto. He quickly bowed, to show his respect, and shambled backward, imitating the gait of a drugged *servus*. But the Regulator kept coming, his black cape sweeping behind him.

Berto's heart hammered. The brand on his arm marked him as a *servus* who had worked in a dig. The Regulator would know immediately that he was a Renegade.

Just then the Follower with the pomaded hair bustled past Berto, apparently unaware that his own *servi* were no longer trailing behind him. Berto grabbed on to the hem of the man's coat and hurried after him, pretending to belong to him.

The Regulator followed for a block, then stopped and turned back, at last convinced by Berto's charade. Berto sighed, feeling a release from the tension wound tightly about him.

He dove into an alcove and looked out, studying the congested streets. Shape-shifting Followers darkened the sky. Their murky forms billowed one over the other like thickly swarming gnats.

After studying the map again, Berto stepped out onto the narrow sidewalk and crept close to the buildings. The roiling clouds didn't seem to bother the few pedestrians walking beside him. They took in long draws of the sooty atmosphere and exhaled blackish puffs, but Berto kept his hand over his nose and tried hard not to breathe deeply.

A mile further on, Berto stared up at a top-floor apartment with high turrets. He glanced at the map again. This was Hawkwick's home. He didn't understand why Hawkwick lived here and not on the Other Side with the master magicians. Hawkwick had conjuring skills and had received special privileges from the Inner Circle, but something must have happened to make him unwelcome in his own group.

An iron staircase spiraled up to Hawkwick's front door, but reason told Berto that Hawkwick would have cast a spell on the steps to stop intruders.

Berto turned his attention to the building next door to Hawkwick's apartment. If Berto could sneak up to the top floor, he might be able to leap from a window onto Hawkwick's roof. He glanced around to make sure no one was watching him, and then he darted into the entryway.

Cobwebs almost completely concealed the

door. Followers seldom used doorways, but waited until they were inside to materialize. As he turned the knob, a long-legged spider crawled over his thumb and scurried away.

The door scraped open, and then he was inside. He waited in the musty-smelling hall until his eyes adjusted to the gloom, and then he started forward.

Lantern flames flickered on, sputtering sparks. The motion-sensitive fires must have been ignited decades back by a landlord with potent power. But the spell had obviously worn away, and the putrid scent of dying magic filled Berto's lungs. He coughed hard, then stopped and pressed himself against the wall, aware the noise might have alerted others to his presence.

More cautious now, he eased down the hallway, brushing his hand over the wall until he came to an entryway. Voices from inside made him pause, and then a shadow spilled out through the keyhole. The apparition stopped, seeming to sense Berto's presence, but the Follower must have had more important business in another place, because the black plume streaked toward the other end of the hall and dove outside through a shuttered window.

Slowly Berto let his body dissolve and join the dark. He slid along the carpet and when he reached the top-floor apartment, he slithered under the door and materialized.

The stale smells of beer and body odor filled the hot, cramped room. Berto spotted a man asleep on a couch. The man's lumpy body made Berto think he had once been a Regulator who had been expelled from the corps.

Berto crept across the room and into an enclosed balcony. The floorboards wobbled under his feet. He opened the window and looked out. The shadows of Followers blurred past him, gliding back and forth like smoky swells on the wind.

The distance to Hawkwick's building seemed too far to jump, and, even if he tried, he'd have to leap through the stream of Followers.

Behind him, the man on the couch stirred.

Berto tensed, knowing he had to make a decision.

"Who's there?" the man called.

Berto weighed his options. He could face the man or dematerialize and float across the narrow expanse.

"Hey," the man shouted, evaporating into a shadow that sped toward Berto. With an explosion of energy, Berto shattered into spinning dots, and his spectral shadow slid out the window, terrified he would collide with one of the Followers traveling past him, but more afraid of the one he had left behind in the apartment.

His vision was panoramic. Even so, he didn't see the dark blotch descend upon him until he was clasped in her arms. He couldn't read her thoughts, but he sensed her trundling through his, luxuriating in memories he would have preferred to keep private.

Her silken voice slipped into his mind. *Hello, Renegade.*

He broke away from her and dove, hoping she would lose interest in him, but she shot after him, caught him, and pulled him to her. Her touch was both exciting and repugnant.

She pulled him deeper and deeper into the hazy traffic, her laughter vibrating through him, and then, without warning, she plunged toward three Regulators standing guard on a street corner.

Tiny blue sparks crackled off the skull of the first one as he turned to look at them. Spiny scales had encrusted his face.

Berto yelled, his voice no more than a hiss of steam. They were going to crash into the Regulator.

CHAPTER EIGHT

JAGGED VEINS of static electricity seared Berto, leaving an unpleasantly bitter smell. The Regulator reached for him, his yellowed bones jutting through the pale scaly skin of his fingers. Berto shuddered and thrashed violently, trying to break free. He didn't want to be captured and become a *servus* again.

The Follower controlling him held him in a tight grip. He thought she was going to release him to the Regulator, but she turned, sweeping Berto with her, and rocketed back up.

Wind raced around them, and then the Follower dropped Berto. His body slammed back together as he hit Hawkwick's roof. Pain shot up his spine. He slid down, over bumpy tiles, until his legs dangled over the ledge. He grabbed a gargoyle's head to stop his fall.

This is where you wanted to be, the Follower whispered across his mind. *No one goes against Hawkwick and survives.*

She flipped backward off the building, and disappeared among the darkened shapes speeding above the street.

Berto swung one leg up and caught his heel in the rain gutter. Already he could feel a change in the airflow behind him and knew other Followers were slowing to gawk at him. If he didn't find shelter soon, one of them would kidnap him and take him on another unwanted adventure, or worse, turn him over for a reward.

He pulled himself onto the roof, still trembling with fear, and made his way up the steeply pitched surface to a dormer window. He touched the frame, expecting a bolt of magic to repel him. When nothing happened, he opened the window and tumbled over the sill into darkness.

The window fell shut with a loud thud. A

short metallic clack followed as the latch snapped into place, trapping him inside. He remained crouching, anticipating the hurried steps of guards, but only silence followed.

He sat in stillness, too defeated to move. He had lost all confidence. What kind of foolish arrogance had made him think he could come into Nefandus by himself and survive? His adventure had turned into a fiasco, and worse than disappointing himself, he had failed his three roommates and the Legend.

Minutes ticked by, and with each passing second his nervousness grew, but so did his resolve. He had nothing to lose. He might as well try. No matter what the cost, he'd attempt to get the book for Ashley, and then, if by chance he did return to earth, he was going to leave L.A. and give up his charade; there was nothing superhero about him. The fates had made a terrible mistake in choosing him.

He stood and strained his vision, trying to see a way out. Fear made his senses sharper, and in spite of the darkness, he saw movement on the far side of the attic. A blackness more sinister than the gloomy shadows crept stealthily toward him, bringing with it the sickening smells of mildew and decay.

Berto sensed intuitively that the creature was one of Hawkwick's enemies, now his slave, forced to live in the attic as a guard to make sure no one gained entry this way; in that same moment, instinct told Berto that the creature, whatever it was now, had been starved and saw Berto as its next meal.

Berto cursed under his breath and darted forward, his feet pounding on the floor.

The large crossbeams that supported the roof were barely visible. He almost hit his head against the first one, then slowed his pace to dodge the next. He didn't want to be knocked unconscious and left easy prey for the creature following him and gaining.

Behind him, the beast sped too quickly and hit the crossbeam with a loud crash that shook the building. Wood shattered and splinters flew about the room in a deadly storm. The creature sagged to the floor, spreading out in a puddle of thick black tar.

Tiles continued falling into the attic until a jagged hole formed that let in a shaft of sunlight.

With the light, Berto was able to see a door. He increased his speed and leaped forward. His fingers grabbed the doorknob, but it didn't turn.

"Come on, come on," he said in panic, trying to find a way to open the door. He pressed his shoulder against the wood, hoping to break through.

He heard a snort and turned.

Yellow eyes flashed open, and the creature pulled itself together in a fierce mass that continued to tighten into the silhouette of a giant wolf. It lifted its snout and released the primal howl of a predator.

Berto fell to his knees and frantically tried to find a loose floorboard to pry free and use as a weapon. He didn't find one, but when he grabbed the doorknob to pull himself up, he touched the filigreed head of a key.

The beast shrieked again, this time in outrage. It leaped forward.

Berto tried to turn the key in the lock, but his fingers shook so badly he dislodged it and sent it spinning across the floor. He dove after the key and landed on his stomach, sliding on top of it.

The creature let out a savage cry of triumph, its lurid eyes hungry and burning with hate.

Berto took the key and lunged back at the door. He fell to his knees again and stuck the key into the keyhole.

The creature's breath steamed around Berto. The stench made him gag, but he didn't look up. He was too afraid of what he might see.

He unlocked and opened the door. But just as relief surged through him, the creature caught his foot and started to pull him back.

Berto struggled forward and kicked off one of his tennis shoes. He fell into the hallway, then stood and threw himself against the door; it closed with a loud bang. He gasped and choked, trying to breathe.

He lay on the plush carpet, still sweating in fear. The homey smells of baking bread and stewing chicken had replaced the attic's stench.

Slowly, he began to relax.

At last he stood and walked down a hallway filled with richly colored tapestries and tables displaying silver pitchers and bowls that looked centuries old. Berto guessed that Hawkwick must have been from medieval times and apparently took pride in his ancestry.

Reaching a set of double doors, he pushed against the elaborately carved wood and eased into a library. Rows of books lined the walls and the room was filled with the musty odor of old parchment and leather. He tried to read the titles on the bindings, but most were written in languages he didn't understand.

A few books were stacked on a large round table in the middle of the room. An open newspaper leaned against these, the prophet's column visible and annotated in red ink. As he leaned closer and started to read, the door behind him swung open.

He dove to the other side of the table and slid behind a high-backed chair upholstered in red velvet.

He heard someone cross the carpet toward him, then stop. Soon after, the room filled with the clattering and clinking of china and silverware, as if someone in a peevish mood were setting the table. Berto peered out from behind the chair.

A girl was arranging a tea service. She placed a strainer over a cup, picked up the teapot, and started to pour. Suddenly, something made her look up.

She caught Berto's gaze.

Alarm cut through him with a stab of adrenaline. He had been careless. He had assumed any *serva* would have been drugged and unable to react quickly.

"Piya?" he asked, guessing that the girl in front of him was the *serva* who had worked with Obie.

She folded her arms over her chest in reply. "Why are *you* here?"

"You're not drugged?" he asked, ignoring her question and wondering why she hadn't taken the potent hana berry juice mandated for all *servi*. But his mind quickly jumped to another thought; she seemed to know who he was.

"I stopped drinking that stuff months back," she answered proudly. "I was going to escape and become a Renegade, like Obie."

"If you've lost your nerve, I can take you back with me when I leave," Berto offered.

"I haven't lost my nerve," she said, indignantly. "I go back and forth all the time. You should know. I saved your life."

"You what?" he asked, certain he hadn't heard her correctly. He stepped out from behind the chair and walked around to her side of the table. He looked down and saw her green high-top sneakers. "*You?* What were you doing to me?"

"You should say thank you." She rolled her eyes to show her exasperation. "You didn't see the bounty hunter coming after you that night outside Quake, so I opened the boundary and pulled you in with me. I kept you hidden until the hunter gave up, then I let you out."

"I remember losing consciousness," Berto said. "I woke up next to the wall."

"I kept you in the boundary too long, and

at first I thought I'd suffocated you," she explained, seeming embarrassed. "You stayed unconscious a long time after we got out."

"That's why you were searching for my heartbeat," he said, trying to make sense of everything that had happened that night. Then he thought of Pete. "Did you accidentally pull another guy into the boundary with us?"

"Do you think I'm an amateur?" she asked.

"But why wouldn't you let me see your face?" He stepped closer to get a better look at her.

"I know how guys work," she said and self-consciously ruffled her fingers through her hair, letting more curls fall into her eyes. "As soon as you had described me to your roommates, Obie would have known who I was, and the four of you would have come charging into Nefandus thinking I needed your help."

"Do you?"

"Do I look like I do?" she answered with a scowl.

He shook his head. That brought a smile to her face. He liked her dimples.

"I had to warn you. I left the flute—"

"How did you know what the flute would mean to me?" He was close enough to her to see the beautiful eyes she kept hidden under her long bangs.

"I study," she answered. "I thought you'd know how serious the message was when you saw the flute. But I suppose it was too much to think you'd actually put the pieces back together and *read* my message."

Her tone implied that she thought he was a fool, but he ignored the insult. Any irritation he might have felt had quickly fallen away, replaced by admiration. He wondered why she had risked so much to warn him.

"When you didn't read it, I had to try again. So I followed you to Hex. But that time, I almost got caught by my master," she continued.

He nodded, remembering the catlike shadow on the fire escape.

"I had to get back here quickly, and I still didn't get to tell you," she said finally.

"What is the danger?" he asked.

"It's too late now," she answered. "If you'd

read the message, you wouldn't be here risking your eternity to help Ashley."

Her response surprised him. "How do you know I'm here for Ashley?" he asked.

A sudden rush of wind against the outside wall made Piya look over her shoulder with a start.

"Double damn," she muttered. "Hide."

"Why?"

She motioned for him to be quiet. Her face went blank in an unconvincing imitation of a drugged *serva*. She poured tea into a cup and nimbly folded a linen napkin.

Footsteps sounded heavily in the hallway. Berto sensed that the person approaching was not another *servus*. He squeezed into a small niche between two towering bookcases just as the door opened. He stole a look, and a gasp caught in his throat.

Hawkwick entered the library, brushing dirt from his cloak before hanging it on a hook. He took off his glasses and wiped the lenses with the tail of his shirt. Mud caked his boots and left tracks on the lush carpet.

What was Hawkwick doing there? Ashley

had said he'd be away. She had made a special point of telling Berto that. Berto tried to find a reasonable explanation for Hawkwick's presence. He refused to believe that Ashley had deceived him, but something deep inside him tore apart.

Hawkwick placed his glasses back on his nose and looked around the room. "Did we have company, Piya?"

A chill rushed through Berto; he pressed back against the wall, knowing he needed to turn to shadow and flee, but his muscles felt too jittery to make the transition.

"Company?" Piya answered. Her act didn't convince Berto, and he doubted she was fooling Hawkwick.

"It's taken you so long to pour my tea I thought perhaps someone had been visiting with you," Hawkwick answered.

"No," Piya said, but Berto could hear the tremor in her voice.

Then the room filled with an odd heaviness. A low and barely audible hum came toward Berto, growing louder. Dust motes rose and twirled in a wispy trail. Berto hunkered down and watched with a growing sense of dread. Obie had told him that Hawkwick used a different kind of vision, but Berto never could have imagined that it would be something strong enough to create air currents.

The dusty cloud surged and then stopped in front of Berto, becoming denser before it fell apart, scattering tiny particles of lint and dirt. Berto pressed a finger hard against the bottom of his nose to keep from sneezing.

"Piya, would you bring me a cookie?" Hawkwick said. "A gingersnap."

As soon as Piya left the room, Hawkwick spoke again. "Berto, please come out. It's unfitting for you to cower on the floor that way. Meet me as a man."

Berto stood and stepped out from his hiding place.

Hawkwick sat in the chair, lifted his feet and placed them on the stool, and let out a deep sigh. He took his cup and sipped the tea with a soft slurping sound, then set it back on its saucer and studied Berto.

"Don't look so surprised." Hawkwick said. "I've been expecting you."

When Berto reached the table, Hawkwick picked up a large green book. "I hate to part with this one," Hawkwick said, smoothing his hand over the tooled leather binding. "But Ashley deserves it: a fair exchange for giving me the opportunity to speak to you alone. I trust you'll give it to her for me."

Berto stared down at the title: *The History of Mesopotamia.* He took the book and threw it across the room. It hit the wall, jarring a portrait of Hawkwick, then thumped onto the thick carpet.

Berto took three deep breaths to calm his nerves and started to dematerialize.

"I wouldn't do that," Hawkwick warned, grinning tauntingly, seeming anxious to watch Berto try.

A force compressed around Berto's shadow. His shoulders sagged under the weight, and his heart began to pound.

Hawkwick held him prisoner.

CHAPTER NINE

"**N**O ONE CAN transform within these rooms unless I will it," Hawkwick said, and walked over to the fallen book. He picked it up, smoothed the rumpled pages, and returned it to the table. "I have simple spells throughout the house to protect my vast collection from burglaries."

Berto pushed against the invisible barricade, trying to break free. But the more he struggled, the more the atmosphere condensed around him, becoming heavier until he couldn't breathe.

"Have you had enough?" Hawkwick asked at last.

Berto nodded, defeated.

Hawkwick waved his hand and the energy field eased.

Berto gasped as the pressure against his chest diminished. But instead of air, his lungs filled with the magic residue falling over him like glittering diamond dust. He coughed and sneezed.

"You seem surprised that Ashley deceived you yet again," Hawkwick said. He picked up a silver tong and added six sugar cubes to his tea. After that he squeezed a lemon slice over the brew. The citrus scent filled the air. "It certainly isn't the first time you've put your trust in her and been disappointed."

Berto didn't know how Hawkwick knew about his relationship with Ashley, but he wasn't going to stay and find out. He moved stiffly toward the door, fighting the pain in his shoulders, legs, and head.

"You shouldn't pursue a girl who will never return your love," Hawkwick said, seeming to speak from experience.

Anger tightened Berto's throat, but he

wasn't sure if he was irritated with Hawkwick or with himself for trusting Ashley. He opened the door and started to leave, knowing the action would vex Hawkwick and make him cast another spell.

"Yaolt Ehecatl," Hawkwick said, evidently indifferent to Berto's attempt to escape. "That's your real name, isn't it? It means 'wind warrior.' Tezcatlipoca whispered the name into your mother's ear at the moment you were conceived, isn't that right? I suppose that means your fate was sealed before you were even born."

Berto paused, his fingers tightening around the doorknob. How could Hawkwick know all this?

"That day on the pyramid," Hawkwick went on, "I'm the one who rescued you from being sacrificed."

Berto turned back. How many times had he wondered what had happened that day? He couldn't leave now. He needed to know. "I don't understand. What are you saying?"

"I think you know exactly what I'm saying,"

Hawkwick answered, his face unreadable. "The priest was going to cut out your heart, but I took you away before he could."

"You stole me from Tezcatlipoca?" Berto asked, not believing this lanky man had the power to defy the gods.

"My colleague Semihazah helped me," Hawkwick said matter-of-factly.

"The demon?" Berto asked, his stomach quivering as repulsion raced through him. He had never met Semihazah, but all *servi* had lived in terror that one day they would. Semihazah was one of three demons created from the cosmic dust.

"Haven't you ever wondered why Regulators and bounty hunters give up so easily when they hunt you?" Hawkwick asked before sipping his tea.

"I'm a strong fighter . . . a warrior. . . . They fear me," Berto said. Panic made the words tumble from his mouth because he was afraid to hear the truth.

"Semihazah marked you," Hawkwick said simply.

"No!" Berto shouted, but already he knew. His hand went automatically to the second scar on his arm. To be the *servus* of a demon was a dreaded fate. He'd heard about the ritualistic abuse. *Servi* were tortured until they surrendered all hope and turned to the Dark One, but Berto had no memory of anything like that happening to him.

"Semihazah hated to see your talents wasted in a death sacrifice," Hawkwick continued. "A true dream walker is such a rarity."

"Did he think my gift would make me a better slave?" Berto blurted out as sudden bitterness gripped him. Such extreme resentment was a new emotion for him and its intensity frightened him.

Unlike most *servi*, Berto had never surrendered his spirit to his captors. He had committed himself to surviving. The masters could do what they wanted to make him suffer, but they couldn't control the way he felt inside. No matter what they did to torment him, he had never let them destroy his goodness and make him like them, soul-dead and vicious.

Hawkwick lowered his glasses, inspecting Berto, and his gaze became more penetrating. An odd spasm crossed Berto's forehead, and he knew Hawkwick was pushing into his mind. The memories of that day on the pyramid came back to Berto with painful speed.

"Stop," Berto pleaded, but Hawkwick continued.

Berto felt himself falling backward in time, reliving days spent with his family and friends. His homesickness became unbearable, and a sad hollowness filled his chest.

At last, Hawkwick left his mind. Memories rippled, then settled, and Berto found himself back in the present moment.

"You wanted to be sacrificed," Hawkwick whispered, appearing unable to comprehend this truth.

"I was the chosen one," Berto answered.

"Please, join me," Hawkwick said and motioned for Berto to take the seat next to him. The invitation was expressed as a command.

Reluctantly Berto took the chair opposite Hawkwick. He clutched the velvet armrests so

Hawkwick wouldn't be able to see the fear trembling through his fingertips.

"Why would you want to die?" Hawkwick whispered.

"Who wouldn't give up their life to save the world?" Berto asked.

"Explain this," Hawkwick said, seeming intrigued.

How could Berto put into words what love was like so that Hawkwick could understand? Hawkwick might have known about passion and the intensity of lust, but as a Follower who would always put himself first, he could never understand selflessness, the largest part of love.

"I wanted to give my life to save my people," Berto said at last.

His words hung oddly between them and before Hawkwick could ask another question, Berto changed the subject. "You could have summoned me a thousand years ago," Berto said. "What is so important that you had to see me now?"

"You need me," Hawkwick said simply, and poured tea into a cup. He set it on a saucer and handed both to Berto. "You didn't then."

Berto gave him a questioning look and took the tea, swallowing the sweet liquid in big, warm gulps.

"I want to be your mentor," Hawkwick announced.

Berto choked and spluttered, spraying tea across the linen tablecloth.

Hawkwick glowered at him. "Someone has to show the four of you how to use your powers before you kill yourselves trying."

"We're doing all right without a mentor," Berto lied. In truth, they desperately needed someone to guide them.

"Why were such fools given these gifts?" Hawkwick muttered; then he settled back and took a deep breath, appearing to collect himself before he continued. "You and your friends know nothing about your destiny."

Berto remained motionless.

"You need a plan, and the only one you have right now is to continue blundering forward into the future until all of you are destroyed," Hawkwick said.

Before Berto could disagree, Hawkwick pointed to the bookcase on the opposite wall. He wagged his finger and the titles on the bindings squirmed, re-forming into English words. On volume after volume, the titles changed to read: *The Legend of the Four.*

Berto gasped, surprised. "So much has been written," he whispered, unable to take his eyes away from the books.

"Scholars study the Legend looking for ways to stop you," Hawkwick explained. "After all, your destiny is to destroy our world."

Berto stared at Hawkwick. "Then why would you want to help us?"

"To claim my place in history," Hawkwick smirked. "Some of us don't feel compelled to sacrifice ourselves for *our* people."

Berto returned Hawkwick's insolent smile. "If you know so much, then why did you let Obie go?" he asked. "You could have stopped the Four from coming together, and then you would have earned a place in history; maybe you would even have received an appointment to the Inner Circle."

"Except that I didn't want to stop you," Hawkwick answered smoothly, and popped a sugar cube in his mouth, obviously taking satisfaction in the astonished look on Berto's face.

"When Obie's aunt Shatri gave him to me," Hawkwick explained, "she wanted me to see if he was a rune master. I knew immediately who he was, but I lied to her. I told her I found nothing special about him."

Berto sensed that Hawkwick felt a deep loathing for Shatri. Maybe he had let Obie escape as a way to get back at her for some past wrong. Followers thrived on vengeance.

"She never would have seen Obie's true destiny," Hawkwick added, "because the death-giving goddess, Hel, protects him."

"The dark goddess," Berto whispered, and he glanced back up at the books on the Legend. According to folklore, the goddess of the dark moon was supposed to help the Four. But even if she couldn't, why would they entrust themselves to someone as selfish as Hawkwick? Moreover, he didn't understand why Hawkwick would offer to help them. Immediately, the answer occurred to him: Hawkwick must have seen some advantage for himself.

"What do you want in return?" Berto asked.

"Ah." Hawkwick seemed pleased with the question and leaned forward. "I want you to go to the astral plane that houses the Akashic Records."

"I've never heard of such a place," Berto answered.

"Perhaps you know it as The Book of Life," Hawkwick said, his excitement growing. "The Akashic Records hold God's history: the thoughts and intentions of each individual since the beginning of time. Can you imagine what a person could do with such knowledge?"

"No," Berto answered honestly.

Hawkwick stood and started across the room. "Come with me."

Berto followed him to an ornate tapestry that covered a wall. Hawkwick pulled it aside, revealing a hidden room. He led Berto to a display case. Beneath the glass were two open books with handwritten pages.

"I have only two volumes. Rarities," Hawkwick explained. "These books were transcribed by a clairvoyant who used the Akashic Records to see both into the future and into the past. As a psychic, he had access to the records, but you, Berto, have the power to actually go there."

"I'm not sure such a place really exists," Berto said. "I've heard that some people just have paranormal abilities like precognition and—"

"But you've already visited there," Hawkwick said, interrupting him. "I saw your memories of it. You encountered the Watchers who protect the records."

"The women warriors?" Berto asked. He had seen the fiercely protective guardians on several different journeys. Once, when he went to an astral plane to rescue Kyle, he had been attacked by them and had barely escaped. "But I thought they were a class of female Regulator patrolling an entrance into Nefandus."

"They protect something far more valuable," Hawkwick said, leading Berto back into the library.

Berto followed after him, gazing up at all the books. With so much knowledge available to Hawkwick, it was hard to imagine what information he needed. Berto didn't know what Hawkwick hoped to gain from the Akashic Records, but he doubted it could be anything good.

"I don't trust you," Berto said, knowing the words might seal his fate. "And I have no intention of going there for you."

"Very well, then," Hawkwick said. He picked up the green, leather-bound book and handed it to Berto. "Don't forget to give this to Ashley. She'll be waiting for it. And I suppose you have much you want to discuss with her, anyway."

Berto took the book, but hesitated, remembering the force field that had enveloped him before.

"You may leave," Hawkwick announced.

But Berto lingered, feeling doubtful.

"Must I show you to the door?" Hawkwick asked.

Berto shook his head, then took one slow

step forward, followed by another, until he was running down the hallway. Why was Hawkwick allowing him to leave? Maybe he was sincere. Could the Sons trust him? They definitely needed a guide, but more than that, Berto wanted to believe that Ashley hadn't deceived him. If she had known all along that Hawkwick wanted to be their mentor, then maybe her deception had actually been an attempt to help him.

But he sensed intuitively that Hawkwick and Ashley had another, more ominous plan, something so terrible that Piya had felt compelled to risk everything to warn Berto not to come. But what had Piya tried to tell him?

IGHT HAD FALLEN in Nefandus, and the red starlight cast a lurid glow over the maze of dirt, bricks, and cobblestones. Berto opened his pocket watch and in its face saw the earth's sky. Time passed differently in the two realms, and he calculated he would return to L.A. at 11:00 A.M., almost three days after he had left.

He crept to the end of the alley. One side of the wall had collapsed into a mound of rubble, but the spot where he normally stepped into the portal looked solid. He wondered briefly why the digging had stopped, but he was more interested in reading Ashley's book. He crouched below a lantern, and in the flickering light he thumbed through the pages, waiting for the portal to open.

Ashley's reason for wanting the book escaped him. The text gave boring details about agriculture along the Tigris and Euphrates Rivers. Anyone could have found the same information on the Internet or in the library. He studied the cover and moved his hands over the leather binding, trying to find a secret compartment. He found nothing, and as he started to read again, a tremor came from the bricks, and he knew the portal was opening.

He stood, clutched the book against his chest, and stepped toward the wall, but a moan from inside made him pull back. Someone was coming through from the other side.

Berto hid behind the stoop as the wall undulated and two figures formed. A large man with a beard and curly hair reeled forward. A girl fell after him. Car keys jangled noisily in the girl's hand, and books spilled from her backpack, landing on the ground with a few soft thumps.

"Courtney?" Berto whispered.

Her head snapped around, and even though she looked at him, her eyes never focused. Without a talisman or a guide, outsiders saw only churning mists in Nefandus. The vapors were a barrier in case someone from the earth realm accidentally stumbled through a portal.

The bearded man plodded back to Courtney, the ground vibrating beneath his heavy steps. His long, bony jaw looked as if it had been broken in a fight. He grabbed Courtney's arm, yanking her to her feet, and with his touch, the world around her came into sharp focus; she was able to see the alleyway.

"Where am I?" she asked.

The man ignored her question and the ones that followed. He braced her against him and started dragging her over the broken bricks.

Berto knew his chances of defeating the man were slim, but he couldn't stand by and do nothing. He rushed after him, crouching low, the book in his hands now a weapon. He leapt and swung, aiming for the man's head, but the man was much bigger than Berto had thought. The book only hit his shoulder.

Berto couldn't stop his own momentum. He tumbled into a ditch and landed on top of the book. Pain shot through him. He lay helplessly, unable to catch his breath, as rocks and dirt continued sliding down on top of him.

"Berto?" Courtney said.

Berto turned. Courtney and the man stared down at him. In one swift movement, the man dropped Courtney, bent down, and yanked Berto's collar, pulling him up in a stranglehold.

Berto tried to dematerialize and flee, but he had depleted his power fighting Hawkwick's invisible force field. His fingers fumbled in the dirt. At last he clasped the book and swung. This time he hit the man on the side of the head. The impact caused the man to loosen his grip, and Berto twisted free. He scrambled from the hole, took Courtney's hand, and guided her to safety on the other side of the alley.

Courtney gazed up at him with a dreamy look of love.

"I'll find an antidote," he promised, gasping for air.

"An antidote for what?" she asked, oblivious to the danger they were in.

"Never mind," he said, wondering why Courtney wasn't afraid when his own body was trembling with fear. "Right now we have to run."

But as they raced around piles of dirt, the man shouted something in a language Berto didn't understand, and then dove with his hands outstretched. He hit a pile of cobblestones and skidded on his belly. His massive fingers clamped Courtney's ankle, and he let out a triumphant scream. He stood and yanked her away from Berto.

She shrieked and fell.

Berto dropped the book, picked up a shovel, and with one quick thrust drove the end into the man's stomach. The man gasped but didn't fall. Berto attacked again, and this time the man lost his balance and hit the ground. Air rushed from his lungs in a loud groan.

Followers were gathering on balconies, and Berto knew that in moments they would join in the fight. He picked up the book and helped Courtney stand.

She brushed her free hand over Berto's cheek, and for a moment he thought she was going to say something corny like *My hero*. Instead, she laughed.

"Why aren't you afraid?" he asked, trying to calm his own jittery heart.

"This has got to be a joke." She composed herself and showed him her palm. Her skin sparkled with the magic residue from Hawkwick's spell. "You're covered with glitter, and you're missing a shoe. Tabitha and Ana set me up, right?"

"I'll explain later," he said, pulling her toward the portal again. "We don't have much time if we're going to get out of here."

"Where is *here*?" she asked, looking up at the tall, narrow buildings rising crookedly overhead. Followers stared down at her. One waved maliciously. "Some new club for psychos?" Courtney said.

"Another world," Berto answered, increasing his speed. Their time had run out.

Her smile faded, replaced with a wide-eyed look of shock. "This can't be real," she said anxiously, reality seeping though her denial.

"It is," he answered. A slight rustle made him glance up. The Followers were fading, and soon their shadow forms would be overwhelming Berto and Courtney.

"Dive!" Berto shouted.

Courtney stopped and stared disbelievingly at him. "Throw myself against the bricks?"

"Trust me," Berto said and pressed his hand forward. The wall rippled as if it were a reflection on water, and the tips of his fingers disappeared inside.

Courtney caught her breath and shook her head. "Okay, you can stop now. This has gone far enough. I want to go home."

"This is the only way to get back," he shouted.

A throaty cough made him turn sharply. The man was standing, and he looked angry.

Berto dropped the book, lifted Courtney, and pushed her into the portal; then he picked up the book, clasped it tightly against him and plunged in after her.

The passing started and muffled Courtney's

screams. Berto tried to reassure her, but before he could reach her, a cold film descended over him, imprisoning him. His body went numb, and his atoms began to rearrange.

Waves rose and fell around him and he knew the man had entered the gateway, but there was nothing he could do now; his body was paralyzed.

Moments later, pain raced through him, and he fell outside, landing clumsily in front of the fortune-teller's shop. He turned to catch Courtney, but she didn't follow after him.

He flung his hand into the portal to rescue her. His fingers hit solid glass.

Sudden and intense grief overcame him. In trying to save Courtney he had condemned her to a horrible death. He imagined her trapped in the boundary, suffocating.

CHAPTER ELEVEN

"**N**O!" BERTO shouted, refusing to surrender to fate. He kicked off his remaining shoe and started running toward Turney High. He needed to find his friends. Obie had the ability to enter Nefandus from any location and didn't have to wait for the demon star to fade. Maybe he also would know how to search through the boundary and rescue Courtney. That was Berto's only hope.

As he jogged past the old men sitting outside the bakery eating sticky buns and drinking coffee, he grabbed a wad of napkins from their table and began rubbing off the glittery residue left from Hawkwick's spell.

Discarded napkins soiled with gleaming dust made a trail behind Berto as he sprinted toward Spring Street. He had depleted his energy in Nefandus, and he no longer had the strength to transform. He barely had the power to move. His body wanted food and a long nap, but in spite of his exhaustion, he ran as fast as he had ever run in his life.

By the time he walked under the freeway overpass, bits of glass and stone had gouged the bottoms of his feet. He slowed his pace, almost limping, and when he reached the other side he was surprised to see Los Angeles Police Department squad cars parked askew, blocking traffic.

A large group of people had gathered on the sidewalk and in the street listening to the mayor speak from behind a tangle of microphones. When the mayor finished, angry voices erupted from the crowd; everyone was unhappy that more wasn't being done to stop the kidnappings.

Berto pushed his way around groups of distressed parents and walked up to the school entrance. Three security guards stood in front of the locked gate, grim expressions on their faces.

"I need to go inside," Berto said.

"The school's in lockdown," the guard answered. "You shouldn't be out here, but now that you are, we can't let you back in. You'll need to call your parents and go home."

Berto nodded. He didn't have time to argue. He turned and charged down to the corner, his anxiety growing. When he was far enough away, he threw Ashley's book over the chain-link fence. It skidded across the blacktop and hit the administrative building with a loud *plunk*. He imagined the school principal stomping outside to investigate the sound, but he couldn't worry about being caught. He took off his jacket and flung it over the razor wire coiled at the top of the fence. After that he started to climb, his fingers and toes squeezing into the spaces in the mesh grids.

At the top, he swung his left leg over, and briefly straddled the fence before bringing his right leg to the other side. The fence wobbled, and he lost his balance. A sharp edge sliced into the side of his foot as he bailed. He landed hard, picked up the book, and took off down the breezeway, blood dripping on the sidewalk behind him.

When he passed the principal's office Tabitha and Ana were standing inside, staring out the window. Their eyes were red and swollen from crying. When they saw Berto, they rushed outside.

"Have you seen Obie?" he asked, impatient to find his friends, but as he took a step away, Ana and Tabitha collapsed against him, sobbing.

He put his arms around them, the weight of the book cramping the fingers in his right hand. He couldn't leave them now, but he also couldn't stop his search. He guided them down the hallway, his gaze vigilant.

"Courtney's been kidnapped," Ana said, her forehead wrinkling in an expression of intense sorrow. "At least, that's what we think happened to her."

"The detectives haven't finished questioning us," Tabitha said, inhaling convulsively. "So we can't go home yet."

"I'm sorry," Berto answered, but his own distress was making his stomach churn.

"The superintendent wants us to talk to counselors, too," Ana put in, wiping at her tears. "As if that's going to help! I'm already traumatized for life."

"What happened?" Berto asked.

"It was Courtney's turn to drive to school," Tabitha explained. "Ana and I had gotten out of the car already, but she was still inside, staring at a picture of you."

Berto wondered vaguely where she had gotten the photo.

"This man stopped us at the stairs," Ana went on. "He wanted us to help him find his daughter, because his wife had just been taken to the hospital."

"As if!" Tabitha said and rolled her eyes. "That's as old as someone telling a kid they need help looking for a lost puppy."

"But you know Courtney," Ana went on. "She got out of the car and talked to him."

"We told her to leave him," Tabitha said with new misery in her eyes. "And then there was a flash like a strobe light and when we turned, Courtney was gone, and circles had been burned around her car."

"Are you certain the ground was scorched?" Berto asked. If his theory was right, the flash and charred concrete meant that Courtney and her abductor had passed into Nefandus around eight in the morning, earth time, and yet they had met Berto at the portal almost three hours later. Why would they have come back and gone through a second time?

"I feel so bad about some of the things I did to her," Ana said. "I wish we could return to this morning and start over."

"We can," Berto exclaimed, feeling a sudden surge of hope.

"What?" Ana asked.

"I just remembered something," he said and rushed off. Ashley knew how to time-travel, and maybe he could convince her to take him back the four or five hours needed to save Courtney.

He hurried around the corner of the administrative building and slammed into Ashley.

"I thought we were going to meet on Olvera Street," she said angrily, and grabbed the book from Berto. She stared down at the scuff marks on the leather, and when she opened the book, dirt sprinkled from the pages. "What did you do to it?"

Berto stole it back and took two steps away from her. "I'll give you the book if you'll take me back in time to this morning," he said. "It's a fair exchange for everything I risked to get the book for you."

"Oh, please," she said, scowling, and held out her hand. "I don't have time for this."

"I need to help Courtney," he pleaded.

"The girl who was kidnapped this morning?" Ashley looked truly surprised. "You think you can stop her abduction? Haven't you figured out anything yet? I thought you had talked to Hawkwick."

"I did," he answered, more baffled than before.

She snatched the book from him. He let her keep it this time.

"Hurry," Berto said, trying to put command

into his voice. "Take me back now, or at least tell me what's going on."

Ashley ignored him. She opened the book and began reading out loud, seeming intent on learning about the canals, aqueducts, and bridges near the Tigris River.

"I'm worried about Courtney," he said and started to grab the book from her again, but as he reached for it tears welled up in Ashley's eyes.

He faltered, then placed his hand on her arm, unable to fathom what was wrong. "Ashley?"

She continued reading in a strident voice. Suddenly, her chin quivered, and she broke into a spasm of crying.

He looked over her shoulder, reading the same page. How could the flow of water into irrigation ditches upset her so deeply?

She snapped the book closed.

"Thank you for getting the book for me," she said, wiping her tears. "I'm sorry I had to lie to you, but I needed this book."

He stared at her, puzzled. He had planned

to confront her about her lie, but her sadness had taken away the force of his anger.

"Berto." She started to say something, a tender look in her eyes, but then she stopped and looked down. "Never mind."

"Ashley, please tell me what's wrong?" he said. "We once shared everything."

"Not everything," she retorted. She turned and left him standing there alone.

CHAPTER TWELVE

BERTO THOUGHT about going after Ashley, but past experience had taught him that he'd hear only lies until she was ready to tell him the truth—*if* she ever was ready.

Thoughts of better times with Ashley came to his mind as he watched her thread her way through the groups of students. He remembered holding and kissing her, and cradling her body against his to protect her from the cold nights at the dig.

Ashley stopped near a bank of lockers and opened the book again, reading out loud. Kids stared at her as they walked by. She slumped against the wall, visibly distressed.

Berto started to go to her, but a hand fell on his shoulder and pulled him back. He spun around. Kyle, Obie, and Samuel stood behind him.

"We've been waiting for you to return," Obie said, smiling broadly. "We'd hoped you were coming back today; if not, I was going to go into Nefandus to find you."

"Do you know who's doing the kidnappings?" Samuel asked, seeming anxious to hear what Berto knew.

"He can tell us later," Kyle said, looking down at the dirt and blood covering Berto's bare toes. "First he needs to clean his feet and find a pair of shoes."

"First I need to rescue Courtney," Berto countered, grateful to see his friends. He glanced in Ashley's direction, but she was gone.

By the time Berto had cleaned the cuts on his feet with peroxide, he had explained everything that had happened.

Obie was the first to speak, his voice echoing oddly in the empty locker room. "If the man who kidnapped Courtney had the power to switch between dimensions, then even if the portal was closing he would still be able to enter the boundary and chase after you. He probably grabbed Courtney before her atoms changed and took her back into Nefandus with him."

Berto hated to think of Courtney enslaved, but at least he hadn't killed her in trying to save her.

"We'll rescue her when we get the others out," Samuel said, with a confidence that Berto didn't feel.

Berto felt even less like a part of the Legend than he had when he'd learned he was one of the Four. He had failed to get the information that he had set out to retrieve, and he'd learned from his roommates that students were still disappearing. The count was up to thirty-seven now.

"I thought you'd be angry when you found out I'd gone into Nefandus alone," Berto said.

Kyle shrugged and handed Berto a pair of ripped tennis shoes and mismatched socks from the Lost-and-Found box. "It didn't take me long to figure out that the three of you didn't want me to go into Nefandus because of the way I still feel about Catty. But I swear, I'm not going to do anything stupid." He smiled mischievously and added, "Not yet anyway."

"But how did you know that's where I'd gone?" Berto asked as he pulled on the socks and stepped into the shoes. "Sometimes I disappear for days."

"Maddie and Emily saw you walk through the window at the fortune-teller's shop," Samuel explained.

"I tried to distract them," Berto said, and felt new worries curl into his chest.

"It's all right," Obie said. "I put another spell on Maddie and a new one on Emily. They think your disappearance was just a magic trick."

Berto stood. The shoes pinched his toes, and the cuts throbbed. "I need to go home and sleep for an entire day, but I want to go back to Nefandus and rescue Courtney."

"We can't leave yet," Kyle said. "The school's in lockdown, remember?"

"It looks more like chaos out there," Obie put in.

"I think we'd better stay," Kyle cautioned. "The kids who are ditching are going to get busted for sure. Besides, I want to hear what the authorities have to say. Maybe they'll actually announce something that can help us."

Berto reluctantly agreed and followed his friends into the noise and confusion outside. Students stood clustered in groups, staring rebelliously at counselors, teachers, and administrators, who were trying to gather them together and move them on to their classes. The vice-principal used a bullhorn to direct students to their fifth-period classes.

"You never finished telling us about the book Ashley wanted you to steal," Samuel said as they neared the biology lab.

"It was really just a way to get me to see Hawkwick," Berto explained. "I realize that now."

"Why did Hawkwick want to see you?" Kyle asked.

"He offered to be our mentor—"

"Never," Obie broke in. "He was a friend of my aunt Shatri. That alone makes him suspect. He's an outcast and considered a traitor in Nefandus. If Followers won't trust him, then what does that say about his deceit and cunning?"

"We need a mentor," Samuel argued. "I do, anyway. I'm tired of cleaning up after a coyote and a bear."

"You love those animals." Berto nudged him. "You named the coyote Jake."

Samuel smiled sheepishly.

But Obie frowned. "We need a mentor, but we can't trust Hawkwick."

"Why would Hawkwick want to help us?" Kyle asked, seeming to have doubts of his own.

"There's a catch," Berto said. "He'll help us in exchange for information that only I can get." Berto told them about the Akashic Records, and, as he finished, an odd sensation wriggled across the back of his neck. He glanced over his shoulder.

Maddie stood behind him, reading a book, but he knew she'd been trying to eavesdrop.

"Is she spying on us?" Berto asked.

"I think so," Kyle said and looked at Obie.

"I'll cast another spell," Obie said, answering his look. "But I can't do it here, and I'm not sure it will help."

"She's just studying," Samuel said defensively, and walked over to Maddie. He kissed her forehead and put his arm around her.

"My spells may be slipping," Obie said in a low voice so no one would overhear. "But there's something more going on with Maddie, and Samuel doesn't see it because he's so in love with her."

"I agree," Berto said, and told them about his encounters with Maddie and Emily the day he had gone through the portal.

Obie nodded. "I cast my runes last night and asked the stones to show me what I needed to know. The stones told me that someone close to me couldn't be trusted." He looked pointedly at Samuel.

"You probably misinterpreted something," Kyle said, following his gaze.

"Maybe," Obie answered, but he didn't sound convinced.

"Samuel would never betray us," Berto said.

"He wouldn't," Obie agreed. "But then I cast the stones again and asked specifically about Maddie."

"And what answer did you get?" Berto asked.

"The stones said that whatever is predestined can't be changed," Obie said.

"You think Maddie is going to betray us?" Kyle asked.

"Isn't it obvious?" Obie said, answering with a question of his own. Then he turned abruptly and left as Maddie, Emily, and Samuel walked toward them.

Maddie stopped in front of Berto. "I've been trying to find you for almost three days now." She smiled sweetly. Her pale hair was combed and hung straight down her back, and when she leaned against Samuel, it caught the sunlight.

"You scared us to death with your disappearing act," Emily added excitedly. "We really thought you had walked through the glass. Did you hear me scream?"

Berto nodded.

"I've got Physics now," Samuel said and kissed Maddie's cheek. "I'll see you after class."

Maddie nodded, and watched Samuel leave; then she and Emily joined the other students filing into biology class.

Kyle and Berto followed the line inside and took their assigned seats in the back, near a bubbling fish tank and some smelly rat cages.

Ms. Beaufort tapped her desk with the edge of a ruler. A large yellow clip held her hair away from her face. She had drawn her eyebrows too high on her forehead, and when she frowned, the black lines folded oddly into her wrinkles.

"Settle down," she said and turned to a diagram of a frog with its chest cut open.

"I can't believe she's going to make us dissect frogs," Maddie complained, carrying her stool over to sit closer to Berto. Her move surprised him, and he shifted his own stool to give her room.

"Not after everything that's happened," Emily agreed, pushing her stool over to join them. "I want to go home. Why won't they let us leave?"

"Half the school ditched," Maddie said, appearing depressed. "I should have, too."

"Where are the counselors?" Emily said loudly. "I need to talk to someone."

"They're taking each class in turn," Ms. Beaufort said too cheerily, evidently trying to infect the students with her own happy mood.

"Great," Emily said. She folded her arms on the table and rested her head on top of them.

Ms. Beaufort started to explain the circulatory system of amphibians as the teaching assistant placed a rubbery-looking frog that smelled of formaldehyde in front of Berto. He felt sick.

"I'm not dissecting this frog," he said. "It should be somewhere under a low shrub, croaking in the mud."

"I agree," Maddie said, smiling at Berto with fondness. "I don't understand why cutting an animal apart is considered education."

"Forget this." Kyle stood abruptly. "I'm going to clean test tubes or empty trash cans."

He followed the teaching assistant back to the storeroom.

Berto sighed. He'd had enough. He didn't think anyone would notice if he stepped from his body. He opened his biology book and fixed his eyes on the page. He stopped listening and became lost in his own thoughts. If the Akashic Records really did exist, then why not use it to his advantage? He and his roommates could have the answers to all their questions about the Legend. And he had many doubts and uncertainties in his life; maybe he could find some solutions to those problems, too.

He relaxed and when he was certain no one was watching, he let his spirit slip out. He floated above the other students and continued through the ceiling. Soon he found himself in the misty corridor, where there were openings into other dimensions. He rose above the cloudy astral plane and journeyed on.

Darkness pressed around him. Apparitions dimmed and blurred about him, some groaning as if lost. Others stared at him hungrily. Even though their presence frightened him, he sensed they were only the confused souls of the newly departed, who were still attached to life and trying to find their way back. He swept away from them, fearful that one might clamp onto his silver cord and use it to slide down to his body and possess it.

In the far distance, a light glowed and drew him forward. The atmosphere brightened, and then he was standing in front of massive marble columns that seemed more dream than real. He moved inside the portico and gazed up at countless stars, densely crowded in layer after shimmering layer, in expanding galaxies, to form the roof.

Berto felt humbled, and he drifted forward, his spirit overcome with deep respect and awe. He was peering into the mind of the universe.

CHAPTER THIRTEEN

ITHOUT WARNING, images and voices spun into Berto's awareness. The Akashic Records were answering all his questions at once, but the information was coming to him in an unintelligible hodgepodge, more nightmare than enlightenment. The spoken words overlapped each other and joined into a harsh, jarring noise.

He wanted to return to his body, but he had lost his bearings and didn't know which direction to take. He floated erratically, terrified he might glide into the limitless stars above him.

How far could he go without breaking his connection to life?

Hawkwick was wrong. It wasn't a simple matter of coming here and asking a question. Risk was involved. Berto had been foolish to assume he could do this. Only the great shamans could.

But the last thought gave him pause. He was the chosen one, the earthly incarnation of Tezcatlipoca. He had been trained in the tradition of his people to travel between the physical and spiritual worlds. He was a dream walker.

He stopped mulling over his problems, and the barrage of voices, writings, signs, and symbols swarming in his mind ended. He thought of the rhythmic clatter that the seashells had made on nights when he had danced through the streets. He began chanting the ancient prayers, and slowly, within his panic, calmness began to grow.

The priests had taught him how to induce a trance and receive the wisdom of the old gods, and he followed their teachings now. He concentrated on a mental picture of the fire within the black obsidian stone. He let other thoughts come and slide away. Soon he was completely absorbed with the image of smoke writhing from the flame within the polished rock. Peace returned to him.

Quiet followed, and he waited, motionless, to receive guidance. A whisper caressed the silence; he listened.

Abruptly the sharp sounds of swords being unsheathed broke his trance. He whirled around.

Watchers had surrounded him, their long hair curling sinuously about their robes. They raised their blades, eyes focused, with perfect determination to sever his tie to life.

Berto willed his spirit to return to his body as he had done so many times in the past, but nothing happened. He tried again. Were these spiritual warriors holding him here?

The captain of the Watchers telepathically communicated the answer: *No one reads the Akashic Records and survives.* Her sword slashed down.

Berto whipped away, but then turned back. He still didn't know the way out.

The Watchers stalked forward, and even

though they were creatures of light, Berto sensed the bloodlust in their resolve to end his life. Blade after blade thrashed down, ripping through the air. Each stroke created a breeze that made his silver cord waver.

He sped, as if in a dream, down vast, endless hallways. As he stepped into another corridor, a jagged bolt of lightning tore through the starry sky. Thunder followed, rumbling through him, and he knew at once he had taken a wrong turn. He was trespassing in a sacred realm in which he didn't belong.

The Watchers raced after him, their long robes flapping wildly.

Berto turned another corner in the maze, and lightning struck in front of him. The vast library filled with eye-burning light; he froze, terrified. Thunder boomed, making the floor shake, and Berto fell against a shelf, toppling some tall ledgers. Old parchment pages rained over him.

The Watchers howled as if he had committed a sacrilege. He had no place left to run. His silver cord made a lazy ribbon, twining around the fallen books. The Watchers stepped toward him with the slow, careful steps of predators who had cornered their prey. The captain lifted her sword, holding it high above her head.

Berto summoned his courage and bowed calmly, acknowledging his defeat. He would not face death without dignity.

The sword came down with a loud *whish*, but before the blade cut the cord, another force yanked on it sharply, and Berto fell forward, tumbling into the middle of the Watchers.

The captain screamed in outrage, and her spiritual warriors surrounded Berto. Blades came down one after the other, but too late—whoever held the other end of the cord tugged hard; Berto plunged back toward life, speeding through the labyrinth of corridors.

An odd vibration shimmied up the tether, and he sensed foreign hands examining it. He had been foolish to leave his body unguarded. His master in Nefandus had made him immortal, but did that mean his body would continue to survive without his spirit?

Then the worst happened. The cord snapped, and his spirit was set free.

CHAPTER FOURTEEN

BERTO'S SPIRIT rose and joined with the souls of the recently departed. He floated toward a brilliant white light, and as he entered that celestial corridor into the world beyond, a feeling of perfect happiness came over him.

Shadowy figures formed in the brightness, a congregation of spirits that he sensed had come to greet him. He saw his mother and cried out in pure joy. She smiled and looked longingly at him, her eyes as gentle and as loving as he remembered.

But when she started to embrace him, a

violent force tore him from her. Berto plummeted backward, down into darkness, screaming his protest. He didn't want to leave the light.

He smashed into his body, and pain spun up his spine. The stool scraped across the floor as he stood and gasped. His spirit beat against his chest, trapped, refusing to settle. It wanted to go back to its home in the light. Waves of nausea washed over him, and for a moment he thought he was going to vomit. Then he passed out.

"Berto, what happened?" a voice called to him.

He struggled back into consciousness and then blinked, trying to open his eyes. He was lying flat on the floor.

Emily leaned over him, patting his cheeks. Kyle stood nervously behind her.

"He fainted," someone yelled. "He's too squeamish to dissect a frog."

An explosion of laughter and giggles burst into the room.

Berto sat up and moaned. Pain throbbed through him, and a terrible headache made him squint.

"Back to your seats, everyone." Ms. Beaufort pushed through the circle of students. "Berto, do you need to see the nurse?" she asked.

"I'm all right," he lied.

Kyle helped him stand and waited for the crowd to scatter before he spoke. "Why did you go dream walking without telling me?" he whispered to Berto.

"I wanted to see if the Akashic Records really existed," Berto answered in a low voice as he grasped the edge of the table to steady himself.

"Do you know how dangerous that was?" Kyle said in hushed tones. "I came back into the room and saw the silver cord dangling through the ceiling and slipping away."

"And my body?" Berto asked, wondering what had happened when the cord had been severed. "Did I look dead?"

"You looked like you were totally absorbed in reading the book in front of you," Kyle answered quietly and turned to make sure no one was listening.

Then another thought occurred to Berto. "How did you get my spirit to come back?"

"I jumped up and grabbed the cord before it disappeared," Kyle said. "Then I ran with it and connected it back to your body. The other kids probably thought I was nuts, but I didn't know what else to do."

"Did you tie the ends back together?" Berto asked, sitting down on the stool.

"I didn't have to," Kyle said. "As soon as the two ends touched, they rejoined."

Berto nodded. But then he thought of his mother, and against his will, hot tears pressed into the corners of his eyes.

"It's beautiful," he whispered.

"What?" Kyle asked.

"The other side," Berto said hoarsely. A mixed feeling of sadness and longing washed through him. "We're going to like it there."

Kyle gave him an understanding smile. "You must have gone too far and stretched the cord until it broke."

"No." Berto shook his head. "I felt someone examining it. Whoever held it pulled on it twice before breaking it. I guess you came into the room after the cord had been snapped in two."

"You mean someone broke it on purpose?" Kyle said, looking around the room for a possible suspect.

"No one could have known what it was," Berto said. "The person must have done it accidentally, thinking they were grabbing a spiderweb."

"Damn," Kyle muttered; Berto followed his gaze.

Maddie held a dissecting knife and was watching them with a curiosity unusual even for her.

"Do you think Maddie did it?" Berto whispered.

"Of course she did," Kyle answered.

"But she must have done it without knowing what she was doing to me," Berto said.

"Don't count on it," Kyle said gloomily.

Maddie plunged her knife into the cork tray that held the frog, then grabbed her backpack and headed for the classroom door.

"Maddie," Ms. Beaufort called after her.

Maddie ignored her and broke into a run.

"I think we've got a problem," Berto said.

CHAPTER FIFTEEN

TWO DAYS LATER, Berto and his roommates sat together in a cramped, high-backed booth in Philippe's Café. Tourists and locals crowded the counter and front dining room as they waited to place orders and pick up their trays. The smells of home-cooked beef and coffee filled the warm air.

"Can we stop talking about Maddie?" Samuel said, clearly annoyed. He set his sandwich down. "I don't understand why the conversation keeps coming back to her. She would never do anything to hurt anyone."

"I don't think she meant to harm me,"

Berto explained. "But I'm trying to figure out what went wrong so it won't happen again."

"The answer is obvious," Samuel countered. "You shouldn't leave your body when so many people are around. Anyone could have grabbed the cord and broken it."

Berto knew Samuel was right, but he also had a strange hunch that something more had been involved, and the feeling wouldn't go away.

"Maddie's been trying to prove the existence of the supernatural for a long time," Berto went on, taking a shot at the topic from a different angle.

"Well, if she does know something," Samuel said, "it's because Obie's spell messed up again. That's the problem, not Maddie."

"I cast another spell on her to make her forget her visit to Nefandus," Obie said. "She shouldn't remember now."

"Did you make sure it was the right one this time?" Samuel asked.

"I'll try again," Obie said. "But Maddie has been avoiding me. I think she's aware of what I'm doing to her."

"You're wrong," Samuel grumbled and spooned more mustard-horseradish onto his sandwich. "What reason would Maddie have to avoid you?"

"Maybe my spells don't work on her for a reason," Obie said, challenging Samuel. "Did you ever consider that?"

Samuel dropped his spoon. "What does that mean?"

"You said yourself that she's always been interested in the supernatural," Obie answered. "Maybe she's explored into the occult deeper than we think."

"*Malleus Maleficarum*," Kyle said in a low voice.

"You're saying she's a witch?" Samuel shouted angrily.

Tourists seated at the next table stared at Samuel, apparently waiting to see what he would do next.

"This isn't the wild frontier," Kyle said calmly. "You can't settle arguments with your fists unless you want the cops involved."

"I'm not talking about the Satan-worshippers

from your day," Obie explained. "But maybe Maddie has committed herself to an ancient religion and has learned how to cast spells to protect herself from mine."

"Wicca," Kyle added. "Nature worship and—"

"Maddie would have told me," Samuel said, interrupting Kyle. "She doesn't keep anything from me."

"Are you sure?" Berto asked.

Samuel pushed back his tray and got up to leave.

Before he took a step, Obie caught his wrist, forcing him to stay. "We need to discuss this," Obie said, his eyes fierce and unwavering. "If Maddie doesn't know how to cast spells to protect herself, then how are you able to kiss her without hurting her?"

Samuel slumped back on the wooden bench in the booth. "I'm careful," he answered quietly, but his voice no longer held a confident tone.

Berto stared at him and sensed Obie and Kyle doing the same.

"Okay," Samuel said, relenting. "You're

only saying things I've thought about before and tried to ignore. But even if she knows something and hasn't told me, what's she going to do with the information? In this town, everyone believes in something screwy. Just look at the irrational explanations people are giving for the kidnappings."

"But if Obie's spell is weakening, we need to fix it," Berto said. "It's not safe for her to know. She might try to go into Nefandus on her own."

Samuel nodded. "I'm taking her to the solar eclipse celebration tonight. There should be a big turnout, so maybe she won't notice if Obie casts another spell on her."

"Pagan is playing," Obie said. "But another band is opening for us so I'll have time to find you before we go on."

"It's really bad that the celebration is being held in Santa Monica," Kyle said. "The beach is right under a portal. More kids will be abducted unless we can prevent it."

"Maybe this will give us a chance to find out what's going on and stop it," Berto said, even though he didn't feel optimistic.

Silence followed, and when Berto looked up, his three roommates were staring at him.

"What aren't you telling me?" Berto asked, not liking the tense expressions on their faces.

"We don't think you should go," Kyle said.

"You've discussed this?" Berto asked, looking from one to the other and knowing that they had. "I'm not staying home."

"If your theory is right, then Courtney and her abductor passed into Nefandus when Tabitha and Ana saw the flash," Samuel said.

Berto nodded in agreement.

"But you met the man and Courtney at the portal almost three hours later," Obie continued. "So it's obvious to us that the kidnapper had been following you and knew what you were doing. He wanted you to see that he had Courtney."

"He was using her as a lure, thinking you'd follow him," Kyle went on. "But you surprised him by trying to take her back with you."

"You mean it was an attempt to trap me?" Berto asked.

"We could be wrong," Samuel said. "But we think it's too dangerous for you to go tonight."

CHAPTER SIXTEEN

THE OCEAN WIND blew the torch flames into blustery spirals and made shadows jump across the spumy waves. Berto walked barefoot in the cold, wet sand. He felt an unpleasant tension in his muscles and knew something bad was about to happen. The border between the two worlds was thinner on this stretch of beach, and he feared that more teens would be abducted during the celebration. His roommates had told him not to come, but he couldn't stay away.

He surveyed the crowd again. Three guys stood on the stage, holding microphones and rapping about the coming solar eclipse. Kids in the audience threw their hands up and moved with the beat, shouting the lyrics back at the performers. Police officers in Bermuda shorts patrolled the water's edge, and more stood near the line of fast-food stands.

Then Berto turned and saw Samuel running up to him.

"I can't find Maddie," Samuel said when he reached Berto. "I told her I'd meet her at our regular spot on the pier, but she's not there."

"She's probably with Emily," Berto said, hoping she hadn't been abducted. "I'll help you find her."

Berto pushed his way toward the stage. Maddie and Emily were big fans of Pagan. Maybe they had already claimed a space in front.

When he neared the speakers, someone tapped him on the back. Before he could turn, Maddie ducked under his arm and stood too close to him, using his body as a shield.

"Samuel's trying to find you," Berto said, puzzled by the way she was acting.

"I know," she answered. "I've been avoiding him, because I need to talk to you."

She grasped his hand and led him behind a concession stand. Smoke wreathed around them, bringing the smells of grilling hamburgers and onions.

"I've been remembering some really weird things," Maddie said, glancing sideways as if she were afraid someone was going to see them together. "About you and me in a strange place."

Berto and his roommates had been right—Obie's spell wasn't holding.

"But that's not even the weirdest thing that's happened to me lately," Maddie continued, talking louder so that he could hear her over the humming generators.

"Tell me," he said, hoping he could keep her with him until Obie, Samuel, and Kyle found them.

"That day in biology class," she said. "I got this picture in my mind that women in gray robes were attacking you with swords."

He looked at her, surprised. How could

she know what had happened to him on the astral plane?

"I knew the only way to save you was to grab the spiderweb floating in front of you." She stopped. "Am I going crazy?"

"No," he answered. "You saved me from the Watchers when you yanked on what you thought was a spiderweb. It was actually a cord connecting my spirit to my body."

"You really did leave your body, then," she said, turning pale.

He placed a comforting hand on her shoulder, but it did not reassure her. Her eyes widened in terror, and for a moment Berto thought she was going to scream.

Then she groaned miserably. "This can't be true," she said.

As she spoke, Obie, Kyle, and Samuel rounded the corner.

Kyle pointed at Maddie, and Obie began to move his hand across the air.

"Don't let Obie take my memories away again," she pleaded. "I need to warn you. If those women warriors weren't some weird hallucination, then I'm becoming clairvoyant, and you're going to face even worse dangers."

Berto turned sharply and shouted to Obie, "Stop!"

One runic inscription already glowed in front of Obie, and he frowned, concentrating on another, apparently unable to hear Berto over the generator's noise.

Maddie cursed and took off, sprinting across the sand, arms pumping at her sides, heading for the back of the stage.

Berto charged the other way, trying to get Obie's attention. But Obie, Kyle, and Samuel were focused on the letters that Obie was writing and clearly didn't hear Berto shouting at them.

The symbols shimmered, casting an eerie orange glow across Obie's face. He drew a circle to strengthen the spell. When the circle was complete, the magic incantation spun after Maddie and pierced her body. She cried out and fell.

Berto went to her, the others trailing after him.

Maddie turned and looked up; a girlish smile had replaced her look of stark fear.

"Can you believe how clumsy I am?" she asked cheerily as she let Berto help her stand.

Then she saw Samuel and waved. She ran to him, throwing herself into his arms, and after that, they walked arm in arm back to the celebration as if nothing had happened.

Berto, Kyle, and Obie followed them. Obie stopped at the edge of the crowd. His band was already onstage. Les and Dacey were tuning their guitars, smiling wickedly at the girls. The audience was becoming restless and had started repeating Obie's name.

"I hate what we did to her," Obie confided. "When I sent the spell, I felt as if I were killing something inside her."

"We went over this," Kyle said. "You had to make her forget for her own safety."

"Logic tells me you're right," Obie said. "But I know it was wrong. Something didn't feel right."

"It's over now," Kyle said.

Berto started to tell them what Maddie had

said, but then he glanced at Maddie leaning against Samuel, all party girl now, laughing and tilting her head in a flirty way, and he decided to wait.

"Let's celebrate," Kyle added, pushing into the crowd.

Obie ran up the stairs to the stage. Girls screamed, and the audience pushed closer. Nolo twirled his sticks and began beating out a rhythm on his drums. Then Les handed Obie his guitar. Obie put the strap over his shoulder and started to play. Les and Dacey joined in, moving up close to the microphone, and the crowd sang along.

Kyle started dancing, sandwiched between two girls from school, and motioned for Berto to join them.

But Berto wasn't in the mood for celebrating. He edged back and hurried away, running down the beach, wondering what Maddie had wanted to tell him. He sensed he would never know until the danger she had foreseen caught up to him.

At the moment he had only one desire. He wanted to be with Ashley.

He ran toward a wooden staircase that led up to the condos where Ashley lived. He hoped she was still home so he could ask her about the book, but even more, he needed to see her.

When he reached the stairs he paused, sensing someone watching him. From the corner of his eye he caught a shadow darker than the others beneath the stairs. He suddenly realized how foolish he had been to leave his friends.

CHAPTER SEVENTEEN

"**B**ERTO.**"** A GIRL peeked out from the darkness under the stairs, and her face caught the pale moonlight. Her brown eyes were large and alluring. He didn't recognize her from school or the club. Still, there was something familiar in her smile.

"Aren't you going to say hi?" she asked. She wore a pink bikini, and had tied a wispy sarong low on her hips. The silky material wrapped gracefully around her legs as she sauntered toward him.

He waited, entranced, and tried to place

her voice. Then he saw the green tennis shoes and gasped.

"Piya?" he said, embarrassed by the choked sound of his voice.

"I borrowed these clothes from a store," she said and twirled around. "Do you like my choice?"

"Of course," he said, struggling to breathe in a normal rhythm. Why was she having such an effect on him? "You look fantastic," he added. A dozen more words came to his mind, but he stayed with just the one. "Fantastic," he repeated softly, and then continued. "Don't you know how much trouble you'll be in if Hawkwick discovers you're missing?"

"I don't care," she said, and gazed down the beach at the couples dancing and holding hands.

Pagan's first song had ended, and Obie started another, his voice strong as it drifted down the strand. The lyrics told of his yearning, but also of his sadness, because he feared he'd never be able to fulfill his desire. Berto knew the song was about Obie's longing to return to his own time, but most of the crowd thought the song was about a girl he had loved and lost. Up and down the beach people lit candles, matches, and lighters and held them up high, as if mourning their own losses. Soon hundreds of flames dotted the night.

"It's so pretty," Piya said, and when she turned back to Berto, her eyes were filled with longing, and he knew the music had stirred something deep inside her.

"Dance with me," she said, and moved closer, the air filling with her fragrant perfume.

Berto put his arms around her waist, but when his fingers touched her bare skin, he felt suddenly shy.

She placed her hands on his shoulders. "One life, one love," she whispered, looking at him.

"That's not the name of the song," Berto countered.

"No, I suppose not," she answered, resting her cheek against his shoulder.

He wondered if she were coming on to him—he didn't want to give her false hope, but at the same time he didn't want to say anything if that wasn't what she was doing.

"Piya," Berto asked. "Why did you come here?"

"I had to warn you that you can't trust Hawkwick no matter what he says or how fatherly he seems," she said, her lips moving against his neck as she spoke.

"I wish you hadn't taken such a risk," Berto said.

"I really like you, Berto," she said.

"I like you, too," he answered in a friendly way, feeling tightness gather in his chest.

"Kiss me."

He dropped his hands and stepped away from her. She was definitely coming on to him.

"You act like I'm being a pest," she said, and brushed her hands through her hair, stretching.

He looked at her body, and when his gaze met hers again, he realized that she had been watching him admire her. He felt his cheeks grow warm with a blush. Why did he feel so flustered? This had never happened before, not even with Ashley.

"I'm already committed to someone," he explained, but his excuse sounded hollow and insincere.

"You've gotten into a bad habit with Ashley," Piya said. "You don't love her any more than she loves you. What you love is your heartache; bad emotion is better than no emotion, and you're afraid of feeling nothing."

"You can't understand," he said. "I love someone else."

She sighed. "I guess that's why I was abducted and taken to Nefandus; I'm only good enough for demons and Followers."

"Is that that what you think?" Berto asked. "It's not true."

She wiped her eyes, and now he felt sorry for her. He hadn't intended to make her cry. He leaned closer, to console her, but he saw that her eyes were dry.

She surprised him by cupping his face in her hands. She held on tightly and stole a kiss. The touch of her lips startled him, and then he felt her tongue. A pleasant ache rushed through him, and his body betrayed him; he returned her embrace, loving her softness pressed against him.

She pulled away before he was ready to let her go, and then she gave him a triumphant smirk, appearing pleased with the effect she had had on him.

"Jeez, Piya, how did you . . . ?" His words fell away. He didn't know how to finish his question.

"I've been practicing my kisses on a mirror, waiting for the day our lips would touch."

He burst out laughing. "You've been practicing on a mirror?"

"It's not like there were any guys around," she answered belligerently. "What was I supposed to do?"

His laughter stopped. "What do you mean, 'waiting for the day our lips would touch'? We just met."

"I guess I know more than you," she said with authority, and started walking down the beach back toward the party, her hips swaying nicely.

He ran after her. "Tell me. No games."

She started to speak, but then, without warning, she grabbed his arm and guided him into a crowd of parents, children, and senior citizens who were waiting for the fireworks display.

"Ashley's on the beach," she said. "I didn't think she'd be back so soon."

"I don't see her," Berto said, looking around.

"I have to tell you about the book Hawkwick gave to you for Ashley," she said, speaking rapidly. "A spell was cast on the pages to hide the information, in case the book was stolen."

Now she had his full attention.

"The true meaning of the words can't be understood by reading them the way you would an ordinary book. The reader must say the words out loud."

"But I listened to Ashley reading the book," he said. "And I didn't hear anything unusual."

"Of course *you* wouldn't," she answered. "It's not as easy as that. You have to be the one saying the words to understand their meaning."

Then Piya slid behind a large man and disappeared into the crowd.

Berto started after her, but Ashley stepped in front of him, holding a half-eaten caramel apple.

"If I didn't know better, I'd swear you were trying to run away from me," Ashley said, offering him a bite. "Let's go to my condo."

Berto knew he should say no, but he was suddenly willing to do anything to make sure Piya got away safely.

"Will you show me the book I gave you?" he asked, returning Ashley's smile.

"I'll do anything you want," she said and the promise in her words wasn't lost on Berto.

CHAPTER EIGHTEEN

BERTO FOLLOWED Ashley through the living room to her bedroom. The window near her bed was open, and the sheer curtains swelled lazily in and out. Ashley struck a match and began lighting a line of white candles set in porcelain holders on her dresser. She hummed a melody from a time long before, and when she held the flame over the last wick, she fell silent, staring into the blaze, as if deep in thought.

In the candle's glow she looked more beautiful than Berto had ever seen her, but also more distressed.

Unmindful, she let the flame burn down to her fingertips.

"Ouch." She dropped the match and shook her hand.

The carpet smoldered where the match had landed. Berto stamped out the smoky fire with his bare foot. Then he took Ashley's hand and tenderly kissed the blister. The taste of caramel apple still lingered on her fingers.

"What's wrong?" he asked, holding her.

"I need to ask you something," she said, seeming unable to find the words to form her question. The anguish in her voice made his stomach drop.

"I can't go back into Nefandus and find another book for you," he said teasingly, trying to brighten her mood.

"You gave me the right one," she said with profound sadness before pulling away from him to sit on the edge of her bed. The book from Hawkwick's library lay on the nightstand beside her.

Berto joined her, sliding one hand around her waist. When he touched her, he was surprised to feel her trembling. Her fear meant only one thing to him, and sudden happiness flowed through him.

"You told the Inner Circle that you weren't going to be a bounty hunter anymore," he said, knowing that it was true. He closed his eyes and held her closer, relishing the moment. Finally, they could be together.

When he opened his eyes again, her lower lip was quivering.

"I had no choice," she said. "Always remember that."

"You made the right one," he answered. "Did Hawkwick's book tell you how to protect yourself from their retaliation?"

"The book told me exactly what I needed to know," she answered slowly.

"My friends and I will help you," he said.

She nervously bit her lower lip before she spoke. "I have something to ask you. Please don't tell me no."

"I haven't heard your question yet," he answered, playing with a strand of her hair.

She drew away from him and stood. "How can you follow the Legend when you don't know what it is?"

"Is that your question?" he asked, wondering why she sounded so angry. "I can't give you a yes or no answer to that."

She knelt in front of him, her hands resting on his thighs. "All you know about the Legend is that the Four will come together and mend what evil has done. Do you really think you're going to be able to destroy Nefandus?"

"I don't know," he answered.

"You fail," she said bluntly. "Why did you commit yourself without knowing?"

"I can't change what destiny has made me," he said simply.

"Defy fate," she pleaded.

"I swore my allegiance to the other three," he said.

"What happens if you break your promise?" she asked.

"I won't. This is who I am," Berto answered. "I'm one of the Four, and nothing can change that."

She stood again and started walking back and forth.

"Then as brothers, they will make a journey into evil's land," Ashley said, evidently reciting something she had read, "and find the black diamond with which they will fulfill their destiny—" She paused. When she continued, she told him something he hadn't heard before. "Four will venture in, but only one will venture out."

He smiled sadly, positive that he understood the source of her anxiety. Now that she had found her freedom, she was worried about losing him.

She stopped and stood in front of him. "Do you think you'll be the one to survive?" she asked.

"I'm immortal," he answered flippantly.

"You know what Regulators can do to Immortals," she said and began pacing again.

He nodded.

"And still you'll honor an oath that you made before you knew what you were swearing to?" When she turned back, she had a desperate look in her eyes that he had never seen before.

"I won't betray the other three," he said and took her hand, drawing her toward him. She was still shivering.

"And what about me?" she asked. Her shoulders slumped.

"I love you." He pulled her down onto his lap. Then, cradling her in his arms, he fell back with her onto the bed. His memory of kissing her awakened a sweet longing. He caressed her, but when his lips touched hers he tasted a tear.

"I know what will happen to you," she whispered, brushing one hand through his hair. "Please, Berto. Make your own destiny, and join evil's side."

He looked at her, baffled, certain he must have heard her wrong. "You said you weren't going to be a bounty hunter anymore."

"I'm not," she answered.

"But then—" He stopped. Piya was right. He was a fool. While he had been interpreting everything Ashley had said as proof of her love for him, she had been scheming, trying to find a way to persuade him to join her and betray his friends.

"If you love me as much as you claim," she said, "then join me."

"Never," he answered and stood, letting go of her.

A soft rustle came from behind him, followed by the sounds of many footsteps on the soft carpet. He didn't need to turn to know that Ashley had betrayed him. He could see it in her eyes.

"If only you had loved me enough," Ashley said unhappily and sat up.

"It's the other way around," Berto answered, holding her gaze. "If only I hadn't loved you as much as I did, I wouldn't be here now, surrendered to the enemy."

When Berto turned and looked behind him, Regulators were still forming in the shadows. They had the power to transform their bodies into movie-star perfection when they came into the earth realm, but they hadn't bothered this time, because obviously they didn't intend to stay. They already had what they had come for.

CHAPTER NINETEEN

ASHLEY TREMBLED uncontrollably, and Berto wondered why she looked so afraid; he was the one in danger. She picked up the book from Hawkwick's library and stepped over to a Regulator with chevrons cut into his cheek.

"I have something that Semihazah wants me to read first," she said, already opening the book and running her finger down the page.

The lead Regulator looked confused but snorted his approval, then folded his burly arms over his massive chest and waited.

Ashley stepped back to Berto. When she reached him, she slammed the book closed and grasped his wrist. Then she vanished, so quickly that her disappearance generated a breeze that blew out the candles.

The force of her change flowed through Berto, and he faded as she pulled him into the air. He didn't understand why Ashley was rescuing him when she had just betrayed him moments before, but he knew that, in helping him, she had also condemned herself to an eternity of punishment inside Nefandus. Why had she made such a sacrifice?

Hellish screams echoed in the room. The Regulators stretched, their faces twisting in savage grimaces as they elongated into nightmarish clouds.

Ashley sped toward the open window and took Berto with her out into the night, her nervousness shuddering through him.

The Regulators streaked after them, a rising black cloud that was gaining on them with deadly speed.

Ashley and Berto spun over the surf, the

salt spray misting through them, then turned back toward the city. Pops, booms, and bangs sounded around them, and the sky erupted with spangled blue, green, and red light as the fireworks display began. The smell and taste of smoke mingled inside Berto, choking him, but he didn't have time to pause. The inky silhouettes of Regulators stormed behind them.

On the beach people pointed at the spectacle, oohing and aahing in surprise and pleasure. Berto glanced back and saw what the crowd was seeing. The shadows of the Regulators gave the illusion of an army charging across the low-hanging clouds. Everyone applauded, yelling their approval of that part of the show.

Ashley and Berto dove through a shower of pink sparks away from the pyrotechnics. They skimmed beneath palm trees on the cliffs above the beach, and after that they sped down Pacific Coast Highway, quickly passing the racing cars and trucks.

Suddenly, Ashley smashed into a bougainvillea growing up the side of an abandoned hotel. Fuchsia flowers cascaded through them as she plunged around the thorny branches toward a broken window. They dropped into a dank cellar and continued through a tunnel smelling of urine, and just when Berto thought he could no longer endure the stench, they burst up through a vent into the night again.

They had lost the Regulators.

Ashley hovered for a moment before continuing lazily down Wilshire Boulevard. When she reached La Brea, she entered the plaza at the Los Angeles County Museum of Art, taking Berto with her.

They remained a web of black, fluttering in the shadows, until a security guard passed. Then Ashley guided Berto inside the building and up a flight of stairs to the exhibit on Mesopotamian art.

Ashley materialized in front of a panel of two figures carved in bas-relief. One appeared to be a king, the other his sentinel. She lovingly moved her hand over the stone. After that, she bent from the waist and shook the flowers from her hair. When she stood up again, she brushed the dirt from the book.

Berto stared at her in disbelief. "Aren't you going to say anything to me?"

"Why? The Regulators were sent to take me prisoner," she answered. "They didn't want you."

"Stop lying, Ashley," Berto said. "Why would they want you?"

"Because I made a wager with Semihazah and lost," she said, staring at the sculpture in front of them. "I bragged when I shouldn't have. I told him your love for me was so strong that I could convince you to turn away from the Four and join evil. But I guess I was wrong."

"What reward would you have received if you had won the bet?" Berto asked, confident that he already knew.

"The power to go home," she said, confirming his guess.

"What made you think—" he began angrily.

"Please, Berto," she said, interrupting him. "Prove your love, and change sides, so I can go home."

"How would that prove my love for you?" he asked. "I'd be here, and you'd be there."

"Do you know what Semihazah will do to me if I fail?" she asked.

He nodded, not wanting to consider her fate. "All Renegades long to go home," Berto said, feeling deep sadness weighing down on him. "But why did your desire make you turn to evil? You weren't always this way."

"I need to return to my own time, because my baby is there," Ashley said simply.

CHAPTER TWENTY

"**Y**OU NEVER MENTIONED a child before." Berto studied Ashley in the museum's dim light. He wondered if she were telling him the truth. Then he looked into her eyes and knew. "You should have told me," Berto said.

"There was too much to tell," she said. "The night I gave birth to my son, three astrologers came to the palace and read the night sky. All agreed. My baby had been born under an unlucky star. He was destined to bring war and death to the world. The only way for me to change his fate was to go into the future and return before the night sun."

Berto sat down on the bench with her and

took her hand. Her fingers were cold, and he sensed her exhaustion.

"I hired other fortune-tellers, but they told me the same thing," Ashley continued. "Then one day, Followers came to me and promised to help."

"But they deceived you, didn't they?" Berto said. "Rather than giving you the magic to go into the future, they took you into Nefandus and sold you to the master at the dig."

She nodded. "Last month I read about the coming solar eclipse. I had to find out if it was the night sun the astrologers had meant. I needed the book from Hawkwick's library. Before I could think of a way to get it, Hawkwick approached me. He asked me to arrange a meeting for him with you. So of course, I said I would in exchange for the book."

"Why didn't you just tell me?" Berto asked. Ashley had started shivering, and he placed both his arms around her, trying to warm her.

"Would you have gone?" she asked.

He shook his head. "What makes the book so important?"

"The pages contain the history of Mesopotamia written two ways: one in which I return and one in which I don't." She opened the book to the page she had been reading when she had become upset on campus. "You can't understand the true meaning of the words by reading them the way you would an ordinary book. You have to say the words aloud, so your soul can listen," Ashley explained, repeating what Piya had already told him.

Berto took the book and began reading about the irrigation ditches in ancient times. His voice rose and came back to him changed. He gasped, amazed by what he had heard; then, with a racing heart, he read faster, hearing words different from the ones forming in his mouth.

Without Ashley, her son would grow up to become a conqueror responsible for the deaths of millions, including the ancestors of Plato, Galileo, and many other greats. The modern world would be different from the one Berto was living in. But if she returned before the coming solar eclipse, the world would remain as it was.

"Now you understand," she said. "My time is running out."

Footsteps and voices came from the stairwell. Guards were running toward them.

"I'm sorry," Ashley said. "I never stopped loving you; when we left Nefandus, I thought I would be returning to my own time. I was shocked to find myself in the future, but when I realized that I was, I had only one goal; I wanted to return to my home for the good of humankind."

"And you didn't care what you did to achieve that goal," Berto said, finishing her thought for her. He understood now why she had become a bounty hunter, but he still didn't approve.

"I had no choice," she said, defending herself. "You would have done the same."

He nodded, because he didn't want to argue with her, but he felt convinced that he could have found another way.

"If I'm successful, everything I did will be justified," she said, as if she had sensed his disapproval.

"But why did you need to go into the future?" Berto asked. "Was there something you had to find to take back with you, like a charm or a talisman?"

"I had to find myself," she said after a long pause. "I'm a different person from the one who left my home so long ago. Through my suffering in the dig, the fates molded me into the person I was always meant to be."

He remembered how kindhearted she had been when he had first met her, how easy she had been to love.

"But you also saw my darker side," she said, looking down at her hands as if ashamed. "I was ruthless as a bounty hunter. That was the way I had behaved before, in the palace."

He understood. She hadn't really changed when she became a bounty hunter; she had reverted to her old behavior.

The security guards were near. Lights had begun blinking as silent alarms went off.

"I need to go back," Ashley said.

Berto stared at her, knowing what she was asking him to do. Then he studied the young man in the sculpture.

"Can you trust Semihazah?" he asked.

"I have to trust him," Ashley said. "There's no other way."

"Then let's go see him," Berto said solemnly.

CHAPTER TWENTY-ONE

SHUTTERED WINDOWS clicked open, and eyes peered out, watching Berto and Ashley walk down the lonely street. No Followers came outside to harass them, and Berto wondered why. When the answer finally came to him, his stomach churned with sickening despair. He and Ashley were marked. Followers knew the demon had claimed them. No one would bother them, because to do so was to risk insulting Semihazah and becoming the victim of the demon's wrath.

"Thank you, Berto," Ashley said, breaking the tense quiet. She looked hopeless in the sputtering light cast from the street lamps. "This was never the way I had planned to go home, but I—"

He caressed her cheek to silence her and was surprised to see the tremor in his own fingers. Her skin was cold, and he wrapped his arm around her shoulders to protect her from the bitter night air. The fires in Nefandus, ignited by magic, burned without warmth, giving off instead a wintry chill. Flames dripped from lanterns, freezing into blue icicles as each small blaze burned out.

Berto tried to comfort Ashley, but fear had made his mouth too dry to speak. In desperation he plucked a piece of hanging ice and put it in his mouth. The icy crystals dissolved into salt. He gagged and spit, expecting to hear muffled laughter from inside the Followers' homes. Instead, the shutters closed, and he knew with dead certainty that even the ungodly felt sorry for him and his miserable fate.

Ashley took his hand and entwined her

fingers with his. He remained silent, trudging on, his bare feet stinging from the freezing cobblestones. He shuddered, knowing what he was about to do. He supposed once he became evil he wouldn't miss his friends or his life, but he wasn't sure that was true. He sensed that evil tormented itself, secretly wishing to be good and, knowing that such a change was impossible, it tried to kill what it couldn't have.

Berto had a grim feeling that he would long for the good. His deadened heart would fill with hungry emptiness and would always envy what he couldn't have. He imagined that, like other Followers, he would try to destroy love and kindness in an attempt to lessen his own misery.

"We're here," Ashley said softly and started to knock on the door.

Berto grabbed her wrist. "I'm not ready," he said in a scratchy, barely audible voice. "We haven't considered everything. If I'm here, then how can the Legend say that the Four will go in—"

"Maybe only three will go in," she said, interrupting, and looked at him with sad understanding. "The future is a collection of probabilities. No one knows for sure what will happen, and even when it seems definite, things change."

He sensed she had more to tell him, but the door opened by itself, and from the end of a colossal hallway, a tall man strode toward them. An elegant black robe flowed around him, making it seem as if the man were walking in a wind.

"Welcome," the man said, smiling broadly. He had caring eyes and handsome features that at any other time would have made Berto trust him.

"Good evening, Semihazah." Ashley tried to return his greeting, but her voice faltered.

Semihazah clasped Berto's hand in both of his. His fingers were tapered and long and bore many signet rings, including three on his thumbs. The seals appeared to come from different empires and eras. Berto assumed that each had been looted as a trophy.

"We were hoping Ashley would bring you to us," Semihazah continued leading them down the corridor.

This jovial man wasn't what Berto had anticipated, but then he assumed that, like Regulators, a demon could change its appearance and become anything it desired.

"Here we are." Semihazah flung open a set of double doors, revealing a massive dining hall. A long table had been set up with a lavish buffet. Steaming baked hams, soups in tureens, and roast pheasant wrapped in bacon sat on platters. A turkey-and-cranberry pie made Berto's stomach rumble hungrily, but then he thought of the starving *servi* in the digs, and a wave of nausea washed over him. The food looked sufficient to feed more than a hundred people, but only Hawkwick sat at the table.

Piya stood beside him, ready to serve, her hair in her eyes. She lifted her head, and the curls fell away from her face. She saw Berto and breathed in sharply.

Berto turned, afraid she might say something, and when he did he noticed the tumbler filled with water. Thirst overcame his other concerns. He sat down and sipped, feeling his throat become soothed. Over the rim of the glass he caught Semihazah watching him, a strange look of pride in the demon's eyes, as if Berto were a new trophy.

"We need to celebrate this moment," Semihazah said, offering Ashley a chair.

Berto had watched Ashley entice the guys at school with the way she slid into the chair at her desk, stretching her legs and letting her skirt rise dangerously close to the top of her thighs, but this time she plopped down gracelessly. She picked up her napkin to spread it over her lap, but her hand shook so badly she knocked over a glass of wine. A purple stain spread over the white tablecloth.

Piya ran and got a cloth, then came back and began sopping up the spill. She glanced at Berto, her eyes intense. He knew she wanted to speak to him, but it was too dangerous. He gave her a look, silently pleading with her to stay quiet.

Semihazah looked at Berto and smiled. "Do you understand what you've agreed to do?"

Berto nodded.

Semihazah leaned closer. "Say it."

Piya looked up and her mouth opened, and for a moment Berto thought she was going to yell for the demon to stop, but then she cast her gaze down, and curls hid her face.

"I agree to turn to evil," Berto said, taking a dreadful oath. "I swear my allegiance to the night."

Semihazah scowled, visibly disappointed with Berto's answer. "What about me?" he asked.

"I give you my soul," Berto whispered weakly, feeling something inside him collapse. He sensed the outrage of the universe over his abominable promise, and knew he had sealed his fate.

China shattered, and everyone at the table turned. Piya stared down at a broken cup; steaming tea pooled around her green tennis shoes.

Hawkwick laughed nervously, as if her clumsiness had embarrassed him. "Piya needs to go home. I believe it's too difficult for her to be around such power as yours," he said, flattering Semihazah.

Then Hawkwick gave Piya a coin marked with his seal to show to Regulators in case she was stopped. The gold piece indicated Hawkwick's consent for her to be out alone. Piya slipped it into her tunic pouch and hurried to the door, staring at Berto. He couldn't tell if her look was one of fear or disgust.

When she left the room, Semihazah turned to Ashley. "You should also leave, Ashley," Semihazah said.

She hesitated, looking confused.

"You're free to return to your own time," he said and waved her away.

Ashley took a deep breath and stood, lingering at the table. "Don't I need something from you first?" she asked Semihazah.

"What we came for," Berto said, with a boldness he didn't feel. "You promised to give her the power so she could return to her own time."

"Imagine yourself home," Semihazah answered. "You've dreamed of it often enough."

"That's all?" she asked, glancing at Berto.

"I hate fools," Semihazah said in a haughty

voice, regarding Ashley with scorn. "You've never needed my help to return to your own time. The Inner Circle gave you that power long ago."

"I didn't know," she said, and stepped toward Berto, her hands reaching for him. "I'm sorry."

Semihazah stood suddenly, keeping them apart. He took Ashley by the arm and pulled her to the far side of the room.

"I was able to prey on your weaknesses," Semihazah said, "and convince you that you couldn't go home without my help."

Ashley kept looking back over her shoulder at Berto.

"You could have returned to Mesopotamia ages ago," Hawkwick said, chuckling and wiping his fingers on a napkin. "You shouldn't have been so afraid to try."

Berto fought the urge to run. He hadn't needed to sacrifice himself after all, but he stayed, afraid of what might happen to Ashley if he left.

"Isn't that the way it always is?" Semihazah

put in joyously and stopped. "Too much self-doubt and fear makes people hesitate and lose out."

Ashley turned and looked at Berto, biting her lip as if she were debating whether to leave or stay and help him.

"Go," Berto said. He sensed that if she hesitated too much Semihazah might change his mind and make her stay.

I love you, she mouthed as a black line appeared behind her. It opened, forming into a tunnel, and then, with a flash of light, she was swept inside. The tunnel disappeared, and powdery dirt puffed into the room, bringing with it desert heat and the fragrance of another, more ancient time.

Berto stood, pushing back his chair, and started toward the empty space where Ashley had been only moments before. He needed to breathe the air in which Ashley had taken her last breath, and feel her lingering essence. He hadn't been able to say good-bye or tell her he loved her.

Hawkwick leaned across the table and

grabbed his arm, stopping him. "We have matters of our own to attend to."

With a savage cry, Berto wrenched himself free and ran across the room. He fell to his knees, robbed of his love and overcome with grief. His chest convulsed in sobs.

Semihazah clasped Berto's shoulder. "I have the cure for this foul emotion you call love," the demon said coldly. "Why bother with it when it always ends in grief?"

CHAPTER TWENTY-TWO

SEMIHAZAH LIFTED his hand and slowly closed his fingers in a fist. A primitive vibration filled the air, and the room grew colder. Berto stood, his heart stammering painfully. His soul would soon belong to the demon.

"It's time to fulfill your promise," Semihazah said. He brought his fist down, and a fire exploded in the dining room. Flames crackled and licked the carpet, leaving a trail of ice as the blaze swept toward Berto.

"Disrobe, and enter the fire," the demon commanded.

Berto had seen the *frigidus ignis*, a ritual ceremony that gave immortality to selected Followers. The cold flames burned away their mortality, bestowing eternal life, but at the same time the fire devoured their souls, making them evil's servants for eternity.

With trembling hands, Berto took off his clothes and stood naked before the fire. Sparks danced around him with dizzying speed. He didn't understand why Followers stepped into the flames with such joy, but he sensed they had been misled, that the truth had been deliberately held from them. Why else would they turn to the ancient evil who ruled Nefandus?

Then Berto caught the sly look in Semihazah's eyes, and terror raced through him. He understood with horrible certainty that this was a secret ceremony, one not sanctified by the Inner Circle or the Atrox.

Semihazah laughed at Berto's fear. "Why should I bow to the Atrox when I can become the lord of evil? I have greater power," he said with growing arrogance. "More skill and cunning, and I'm not the only one tired of waiting.

The Atrox holds the Daughters of the Moon captive, and it hesitates, not ready to destroy them."

In response to Semihazah's rage, the fire burst into a larger conflagration. Ice encrusted the ceiling and chandeliers. Berto shivered, his face and body stinging from the cold. Flames hissed, sputtered, and curled over his feet, then moved up and around his knees.

Through the veil of flames Berto watched Semihazah watching him. What could such a powerful demon want with him? And then, bit by bit, he figured it out; Semihazah couldn't travel to the astral plane as Berto could. The demon needed him for that.

Without warning, Berto's spirit started to leave his body, drawn out by another force. At first he thought Semihazah was doing this to him, but then he realized that his spirit was being called upward to the regions above this plane.

Flames shot after him, twisting around the silver cord and trying to make his spirit stay, but a stronger power pulled him forward.

Soon, silence and soothing darkness engulfed him. He waited, in a great void, and, from the emptiness, a figure formed and walked toward him. The man was adorned in flowers and seashells; his features were sharp. He wore a net cape decorated with human skulls that clattered against each other in a slow, even rhythm.

He stopped, and Berto stared into the face of Tezcatlipoca.

"Yaolt." The god called Berto by his Toltec name and handed him the smoking mirror. The obsidian stone gave clairvoyance to anyone who was allowed to look into it.

The smoke cleared, and Berto saw his own reflection. He was still the chosen one, his destiny awaiting him. He bowed his head, determined to prove himself worthy.

Tezcatlipoca took off a seashell necklace and slipped it over Berto's head. "This will protect the soul within your spirit," he said.

After that, Tezcatlipoca placed one hand on Berto's shoulder and pushed him back through the churning smoke into life.

Berto fell into his body. Pain shuddered through him, and he let out a savage cry; he wanted to return to his lord and stay in the land of the dead. He blinked. His vision returned, and slowly the room came into focus.

The fire had died out, and Berto stood on the surface of a frozen puddle, shivering. He took one careful step forward, and ice crunched beneath his bare feet.

Hawkwick shook out a large, floor-length cape and with a flourish wrapped it around Berto's shoulders.

"I didn't think I'd ever get warm again after my ceremony," Hawkwick said good-naturedly.

Berto remembered the seashell necklace and brought his hand up, suddenly afraid Semihazah and Hawkwick would see it and take it from him. He patted his chest, but the necklace was gone. Then he remembered that Tezcatlipoca had slipped it over his spirit self; the charm rested inside him, encircling his soul.

"Your chest feels hollow without a soul, doesn't it?" Hawkwick said, misinterpreting

Berto's movement. "You'll get use to it. I have."

"So many converts have told me the same," Semihazah added. "Although I wouldn't know, because I never possessed my own."

"You've joined our brotherhood," Hawkwick said in confidence, even though they were the only three in the room. "Now we'll share our darkest secret with you."

Berto didn't want to hear. He started to reach for his clothes.

"Follow us," Semihazah ordered, already transforming into a column of black.

Semihazah and Hawkwick didn't wait for Berto to dress. They sped away, two ghostly shadows racing, one after the other, down the hallway.

Berto hurriedly bundled up his clothes. He was naked, freezing, and his head pounded. He wanted nothing more than to dress, climb under a pile of blankets and take a long nap, but he fought his exhaustion, dematerialized, and sped after them.

Semihazah and Hawkwick flowed swiftly down to the cellar, two phantoms disappearing into the dark. Berto streamed after them. He sensed they were taking a secret route, so that neighbors wouldn't see them leave the house and wonder where they were going.

When finally they left the underground passageway they were far from the city. They flew over rugged terrain and continued past marshy grasslands flooded with salt water. Then Semihazah soared, a streak of black spiraling up toward a chain of mountains—five peaks pointed toward the sky, the shortest one opposing the other four, with the curious look of a human hand. Hawkwick followed close behind, and Berto glided after them, sailing higher and higher on the rising currents.

Semihazah and Hawkwick had already materialized on a ledge above the ocean by the time Berto drifted down and joined them. Berto became visible near the mouth of a cave. He wrapped the cape around his naked body and unfolded his clothes, but as he started to step into his boxer shorts, he stopped.

From the depths of the cavern beside him came the clang of metal hitting solid rock.

Berto recognized the moans and sighs of suffering that followed. His deception had been discovered. Semihazah had known all along and had brought him to a dig, where he would be imprisoned.

Berto collapsed against the rocks, remembering the labor with aching clarity, the way his skin had ripped from his palms during those first days spent digging. He didn't know if he could endure the branding iron and the vicious whippings again.

He looked out at the ocean, sparkling with the reflection of the red stars, and stepped to the edge of the cliff. The surf crashed over the jagged rocks below him. He held out his hand and caught the salty spray. He wanted one last moment of freedom. He turned, defeated, expecting Hawkwick to hand him a vial of hana berry juice. He almost welcomed it as a way to escape the terror and have the night over.

CHAPTER TWENTY-THREE

BERTO REMAINED motionless, struggling to breathe. He started to cry out, but Hawkwick spoke first.

"This is where we suspect the black diamond has hidden itself," Hawkwick said enthusiastically, and clasped Berto's shoulder.

"What?" Berto asked, confused, and then he looked at Hawkwick and Semihazah. He had expected to see their wrath. Instead, they were smiling. They hadn't figured out yet that Berto had deceived them. Relief flooded through him, and he smiled foolishly, feeling jubilant.

"Ahhh," Hawkwick sighed in a self-satisfied way. "I can see from your excitement that you have some idea why we have brought you here."

Berto didn't have a clue, but he knew better than to let on. He felt deliriously happy that he wasn't being consigned to a dig.

"Let me explain," Hawkwick said as if they were conspiring. "This flat terrain between the peaks is called the Devil's Palm for obvious reasons. Now, look." He pointed toward the forest. "What does that remind you of?"

The stars lit the moonless night and cast a burgundy glow over the verdant woodland behind them, but in the dry land near the cave the trees were dead. Their branches jutted up toward the sky with an odd resemblance to antlers.

"Elk horns," Berto said, understanding at last.

"Exactly," Hawkwick exclaimed, seeming proud of himself. "The Oracle said the diamond had concealed itself where the elk horns crossed the devil's palm. Everyone searched for the obvious, but I'm convinced they misinterpreted what the Oracle said. Clearly, this is far more likely the resting place of the diamond than the crossroads of two city streets."

"Far more likely," Semihazah said. His bored tone suggested that Hawkwick had talked excessively about his brilliant reasoning.

"You're searching for the black diamond like everyone else," Berto said, surprised.

"Definitely *not* like everyone else," Hawkwick countered.

Then Berto remembered the abandoned ditches in the street near the portal. "Why did the others give up their search?"

"The Atrox has become suspicious," Semihazah explained. "It called off all searches except for the ones it sanctioned—"

"Then what we're doing is illegal," Berto said with rising uneasiness.

"It's illegal only if we're caught," Semihazah said slyly.

"The Atrox suspects treason—" Hawkwick began.

"How could anyone call my acts treasonous?" Semihazah said, interrupting Hawkwick. "The Atrox is the traitor. It has the Daughters! The goddesses have always been the only ones who stood in our way. We can destroy humankind now, so why is it hesitating? We need the black diamond to defeat the Atrox, and the sooner the better."

Hawkwick looked nervously about. "We have to find the diamond soon," he agreed quietly. "I read in the newspaper that Regulators are combing the countryside looking for illegal digs."

"Why do Regulators remain so loyal to the Atrox?" Semihazah fumed. "I don't understand their devotion. Of all the residents of Nefandus, they should be the ones to rebel. Just being around the Atrox turns their bodies to mush."

He threw his hands into the air and screamed wretchedly. The high-pitched noise echoed into the night. Then a lightning bolt crackled from the tips of his fingers and shot across the sky, defusing his anger.

"Well," Hawkwick added with a shrug. "Enough said for now. Perhaps we should go inside."

Semihazah turned abruptly and marched into the tunnel. Hawkwick headed after him.

Reluctantly Berto wrapped the cape around his body and followed them into complete blackness. Rocks cut painfully into his soles. He tripped and scraped his palm on the cavern wall. Stones and dirt poured over his fingers in a small avalanche from overhead.

"I think we have a more immediate problem," Berto said into the darkness.

"What now?" Semihazah yelled back, clearly agitated.

"You didn't brace the tunnel with timbers or magic," Berto explained. "It could collapse."

"We can't use too much magic here," Semihazah said impatiently. "The energy emitted when magic is performed sends out waves that Regulators can sense. I can't do more. I've already used too much on the spells to light the lanterns."

If any lanterns had been lit, Berto couldn't

see their light, but he did feel the tension gathering around him in the dark.

"End of topic," Hawkwick whispered.

Berto nodded, even though he doubted Hawkwick could see his gesture. He stepped forward following the sound of Hawkwick's footsteps.

A short time later, lantern flames flickered and lit the narrow passage. In the dim light Berto saw sand and pebbles sifting through long, narrow cracks overhead. In some areas the sides had already collapsed, and rocks lay in piles. The tunnel needed to be reinforced; *servi* could do that without magic. If the diamond were here, Berto sensed that Semihazah was destroying his chances of finding it because in his urgency to get it, he was being too reckless. The tunnel was going to cave in soon.

Berto started to warn Hawkwick and Semihazah about the danger again, but when he stepped around the next bend, he fell into a huge mound of dirt. He climbed over it and realized they had reached the bottom of the cavern. He wasn't prepared for what he saw.

Kids his age toiled in a deep ditch the size of a football field. Some were crying, others cursing, but all looked distressed; they had the vacant stare of the damned. Thin gold bands encircled their necks. The shackles marked them as newly arrived *servi* and gave them the ability to see in Nefandus, but the fetters were also used to train them to work relentlessly. He watched as the girl below him paused to stretch her back. The collar tightened, choking her, and she immediately began loading dirt into a wagon again.

Berto recognized most of the kids from the club and school. Pete was in the group, shoveling hard. He had taken off his rhinestone-studded jacket and tied it around his waist. His dyed-white hair was now a reddish brown, from working in the clay dirt.

"Did you make them immortal?" Berto asked.

"Hardly," Hawkwick answered. "We told you this dig isn't sanctioned, so how could we hire someone to do that?"

"But you have magic—" Berto began.

Hawkwick's laughter interrupted him. It implied that he clearly thought such magic was beneath him. *Servi* didn't receive immortality through the *frigidus ignis* ceremony. Their souls were left intact. A lesser magician took away their mortality for a fee.

Someone whimpered in the pit below him. Berto looked over the edge and saw Courtney. She was rubbing her arm, obviously in pain. The gold collar pinched her neck and she started picking up large stones again, setting them in a pile. He turned quickly so she couldn't see his face.

"You knew we had Courtney," Hawkwick said. "We brought her through the boundary twice to make sure that you did. With Ashley gone, we didn't want you to think you could defy us." He grinned as if he thought his strategy were bordering on genius.

Berto nodded, understanding. Followers never relied on trust, because they only saw in others what they held inside their own hearts. He supposed Semihazah and Hawkwick feared that Berto would find the diamond and keep it for himself, but he didn't consider their motivation for long. He was more concerned about the kids in the dig.

"And what about the hana berry juice?" Berto asked. "How do you get enough down here?"

"We don't," Hawkwick said.

"Why bother?" Semihazah smirked. "When these *servi* expire, we'll toss them back through the portal and get new ones. Let the police officers and coroners puzzle over their deaths."

Berto took a deep breath trying to calm himself. He didn't understand why he felt so suddenly afraid, but then he realized he wasn't concerned for his own safely. He was worried about the kids in the pit. How was he going to get them back to L.A. alive?

"You have such great powers," Berto said to Semihazah, making one last desperate attempt. "Why don't you use your magic and make the diamond come to you? We can still get away before the Regulators show up."

Semihazah gave him a dismissive look. "If

the diamond has the power over all the magic in the universe, do you actually think it would succumb to a spell, even one as strong as mine?"

"The more powerful one's magic is, the more dangerous it is to use it to find the diamond," Hawkwick explained, flattering Semihazah and trying to calm him. "The diamond deflects any spell cast upon it, and fires the spell back at the magician who sent it. The gem has developed a will of its own and has already destroyed several master magicians who were searching for it."

"Then how can we obtain the diamond?" Berto asked, knowing Semihazah wouldn't release the kids in the dig until the diamond was located.

"That's for you to find out," Semihazah said and smiled at Berto.

"Me?" Adrenaline shot through Berto, and he felt his heart race in response.

"We want you to go to the Akashic Records," Hawkwick said. "You'll be able to learn the precise location of the diamond."

"But what if the information isn't there?" Berto asked.

"I will have that diamond!" Semihazah shouted. "I am going to dethrone the Atrox, and I promise to destroy anyone who stands in my way." He glared at Berto, evil gleaming in his eyes. Berto could feel hatred coming off the demon in waves.

"I'll get the information," Berto said, not sure he could.

"Be prepared to face extinction if you don't," Semihazah warned him.

CHAPTER TWENTY-FOUR

ERTO STEPPED BEHIND the dirt piled near the entrance to the cavern, trying to summon his courage. He didn't want anyone to watch him leave except for Hawkwick and Semihazah, and at the same time he had a bad feeling about entrusting them with his vacated body. He worried that when he returned—if he did—he would find another entity inhabiting what had once been his flesh and bones.

He clasped his hands together to stop their trembling, then closed his eyes and focused. He sensed Semihazah and Hawkwick staring at him.

"I need privacy," Berto said, but in fact he feared they might see the seashell necklace that Tezcatlipoca had tied around his spirit.

"You're wasting time," Hawkwick muttered, stepping back. "We need to hurry."

"Do it now," Semihazah demanded, and scraped a jagged fingernail down Berto's neck.

"All right," Berto shouted and with a painful shudder, he left his body. He could feel his heartbeat pulsing up the silver cord and knew he had separated too quickly.

He slipped through layers of dirt, up and out into the night. Soon he was traveling in the heavenly sphere toward the Akashic Records. This time, when he arrived, instead of floating up the stairs as he had done before, he hovered in front of the portico, mulling over his dilemma.

Minutes ticked by, and still he didn't know what to do. Berto sensed it must be an offense to the universe to use the Akashic Records to find the black diamond, but even if it wasn't a sacrilege, he didn't want to give Semihazah its location. Once the demon found the gem, he would use it to destroy humankind.

On the other hand, Berto feared that if he didn't return with the information, Semihazah would harm the kidnapped teens. Berto felt hopeless. He had no options. In order to save the world, he had to sacrifice his own life and the lives of those digging in the cavern. He needed guidance.

All at once a white light washed over him, and within the middle of the brightness, a door appeared, suspended in the air. It opened, and a voice from inside called to him, inviting him to enter.

As soon as he crossed the threshold, the light quivered through him. The overwhelming power of the universe was putting thoughts into his mind. The answers started to penetrate his spirit, but before he received everything he needed to know, someone tugged on the silver cord.

"No!" Berto screamed, too late. He was already falling away from the light. He plummeted down, wind shrieking around him.

He was still screaming when his spirit slammed into his body. The pain was intense. He lost consciousness, and when he opened his eyes again Semihazah and Hawkwick were staring down at him in anticipation.

Berto stood, his muscles aching as his spirit tried to settle. "You pulled me back too soon," he said, feeling cheated; he wanted to return to the light.

"You had enough time. You were gone for almost an hour," Semihazah said. Then a frown replaced his confident expression. "You didn't retrieve what I requested."

"No," Berto answered.

Semihazah leaned closer, his eyes piercing. "You didn't even try, did you?" he said, his jaw clenching in rage.

Berto rubbed his forehead against the beginning of a piercing headache and didn't answer Semihazah's question.

"You deceived us in the fire," Semihazah

continued, grasping the truth. "Why didn't I see this before?"

"That's impossible," Hawkwick said. "I saw the fire crust over him with ice. He couldn't have misled us. He wouldn't betray us."

"He did," Semihazah said. "He's a dream walker. His spirit abandoned his body during the ceremony."

Hawkwick took off his glasses and stared at Berto. "You're immortal, so you know there are fates worse than death. Why would you risk eternal torture to save your soul?"

"I could never make a Follower understand," Berto said.

"I'll give you what mortals fear most," Semihazah said, and he raised his hand, his fingers tight together. In the center of his palm a fire sparked, and from it, a venomous vapor snaked into the air, writhing toward Berto.

"Once you breathe the smoke," Semihazah explained, "you'll begin suffering the pain of dying . . . for eternity."

Berto stood defiantly still, refusing to give the demon the pleasure of his fear.

CHAPTER TWENTY-FIVE

LOUD VOICES and pounding footsteps echoed into the cavern from the tunnel. Semihazah brought his hand down and staggered back, his look of anger turning into one of pure astonishment.

"What are they?" he asked, and glanced at Hawkwick as if seeking an explanation.

"Fools," Hawkwick scoffed.

The black mist evaporated, and Berto turned, taking in a deep breath and getting ready to run. He expected to see a legion of Regulators. Instead, Samuel, Obie, and Kyle stumbled down the pile of dirt, knocking into each other as they struggled to stand. Samuel wore baggy gym shorts and a T-shirt. His hair was standing on end. Kyle was still dressed in pajama bottoms, his eyes groggy. Obie was wearing jeans and appeared exhausted. Berto guessed Obie looked so drained because he had used his ability to shift between dimensions to bring the others into Nefandus.

"Hawkwick is right about one thing," Berto said when they joined him. "You were fools to come here, but I'm glad you did."

"Looks like we're not the only fools," Samuel said, staring at Berto in disbelief. "What is that outfit you're wearing . . . or not wearing?"

Berto wrapped the cape around his nakedness. "I think I left my jeans somewhere near the entrance."

"Why?" Kyle asked, shaking his head and snickering.

"Long story," Berto answered and started

to explain. But Samuel nudged him and pointed.

Hawkwick and Semihazah were glaring at them.

Berto felt his heart sink. His friends were acting brave, attempting to give the impression that they weren't afraid, but both Hawkwick and Semihazah had incredible powers, and Berto feared that, far from rescuing him, his friends had condemned themselves to suffer a terrible fate.

"Meet the Four of Legend," Hawkwick said derisively.

"This is what the members of the Inner Circle fear?" Semihazah asked before he broke into malicious laughter.

"His reception isn't making me feel good about our powers," Obie said.

"We need a mentor," Samuel put in. "Everyone in Nefandus is afraid of us until they meet us. What gives?"

"We don't need a mentor," Kyle insisted. "We just need to stage a terrifying entrance."

"Right," Berto said. "If we escape this,

then you can choreograph something for us."

"What are they doing now?" Samuel asked.

Semihazah and Hawkwick had backed away and were leaning against the cavern wall, arms folded over their chests.

"I think they're waiting for us to entertain them," Kyle answered.

"Show me what you've learned, Obie," Hawkwick taunted. "Have you followed your heritage and become a rune master yet?"

"I'm doing all right," Obie answered, but he didn't hide his reluctance to fight Hawkwick.

Berto sensed Obie's terror and wondered what Hawkwick had done to him during the years Obie had been his *servus*.

"What's wrong?" Samuel asked.

"I've seen what Hawkwick can do," Obie whispered and swallowed hard. "I can't fight his magic."

"We're waiting, Obie," Hawkwick said gleefully.

Semihazah snorted, seeming to have

forgotten about his quest for the black diamond.

"I'll take care of this," Kyle said and
squinted, his concentration clearly intense.

The atmosphere buckled and bent, distort-
ing everything, and then, in rhythmic bursts,
golden scales formed a body with a long tail and
neck. After that, black reptilian eyes blinked,
and the ferocious mouth of a tyrannosaur
opened, exposing sharp teeth.

Warm air ruffled though Berto's hair, and
he stepped back, astonished. The beast was
breathing.

It emitted a loud, growling noise and
stepped forward. The ground trembled beneath
its huge, clawed feet. It twisted its head and
focused on Semihazah.

Undaunted, Semihazah raised his hand to
summon a beast of his own, but stopped when
Kyle's creature paused. The giant reptile
sniffed, and then uttered a harsh cry of distress
as its head fell and it began shedding scales. A
ripple washed down its back, followed closely by
another.

"I'm losing him," Kyle yelled, visibly shaken and trying to maintain his focus.

"Take cover!" Samuel cried.

In that instant, the creature turned into ectoplasm and a flash flood of greenish gray slime washed through the cavern, swamping Semihazah and Hawkwick, splashing against the walls, and churning back in a wave toward Berto.

Berto opened his mouth to warn the others to run to higher ground, but the wave slapped him, filling his mouth. The thick, slippery liquid curled over and around his tongue like a mouthful of slugs, tasting worse than it smelled. He spat and gagged as the flood receded, dripping into the ditch.

"Man, don't do that again until you've practiced more with little things," Berto yelled at Kyle, then spat again, wanting to retch as bile rose to the back of his throat.

Screams and yells of disgust came from the pit behind them.

"Sorry," Kyle said, wiping the icky stuff from his own face.

Semihazah levitated above the oozing mess, his hair matted with the gray-green muck. His expression was a mixture of revulsion and rage. He lifted his hand to cast a spell on Kyle.

Obie dove in front of Kyle and marked a line of runic symbols in the air. The two spells crashed, sending a flurry of sparks into the cavern.

Semihazah turned and focused his attention on Obie.

"Don't," Hawkwick said, breathless. He struggled toward Semihazah and caught his wrist. "Be careful. Your power is too strong. Regulators will be able to feel the energy coming from your magic."

Semihazah paused and stared blankly. Berto knew at once he was searching with his mind, gazing into the night with a stronger vision than that of his eyes.

"They're coming," Semihazah said, and then he looked at the Four.

"There's no way we're getting out of here alive," Kyle muttered.

"Of course there is," Obie joked. "We're Immortals. They can't kill us."

"Maybe he's afraid of coyotes," Samuel suggested; he touched the carving of the coyote that hung from his neck on a thin piece of leather.

"Get real," Kyle answered. "Even I'm not afraid of your coyote. Do you think flea bites will stop these guys?"

"It's too late now," Samuel answered.

The coyote dropped from the air, landing in the dirt with a loud *thunk*. It yowled in protest, and then curled into a ball, preparing to sleep.

"Attack!" Samuel yelled. "Come on, Jake. Show these guys what you're made of."

The coyote stood and shook its head, then sniffed the air, whimpered, and scuttled behind Samuel.

"It's our last chance," Samuel said, clasping his totem of the mountain lion.

"Don't," Berto warned. "You don't have any control over that. I have a better idea."

"You mean run?" Kyle asked. "I'm game for that."

"Enough," Semihazah screamed, his eyes

filled with hatred and a need for revenge. Silence, except for the soft sound of shovels scraping into dirt, filled the cavern. "I will not have my plans ruined without getting my revenge."

"Then take me," Berto said, stepping forward. "And let my friends go."

"Be careful," Hawkwick warned.

"Of what?" Semihazah said with contempt. "These boys?"

"The Legend," Hawkwick whispered. "The diamond can overhear you, and you know its connection to the Four."

"If these are the Four, then I have nothing to fear from the diamond or the future. I've already marked this one." With that, Semihazah raised his hand, and one by one he folded his fingers down onto his palm.

A terrible pressure tightened around Berto's chest. His heartbeat slowed, and he could feel the pulse thumping in his ears, each beat slower than the last. Then Semihazah clenched his fist.

Berto gasped and fell to his knees.

CHAPTER TWENTY-SIX

THE COYOTE SNARLED, baring its teeth, and lunged, transformed into a beautifully ferocious beast. It swept through the air and attacked Semihazah's hand, biting his fist hard until Semihazah's fingers opened and the spell broke.

"Thanks, Jake," Berto said, rubbing his chest. His lungs felt as if they were on fire, and his legs throbbed as he struggled to stand.

Samuel and Kyle ran to him and pulled him up. "I bet you'll never complain about flea bites again," Samuel said.

Berto nodded, but his attention was drawn back to Semihazah.

The demon shrieked, trying to free himself from the coyote. He lifted his hand to hex the animal, and when he did, he lost his balance and stumbled back into a puddle. Water splashed over him, and a strange, startled look crossed his face. He lifted the hem of his robe and stared down at his feet. He struggled to step from the swampy water, but every time he moved, he sank deeper.

A deadly cold swept through the cavern. The coyote yelped and backed away, tail curled between its legs.

"What did he do to Jake?" Samuel asked, moving forward.

Berto caught Samuel's arm and pulled him back. "Semihazah didn't hurt Jake. Something else is going on."

Semihazah frowned and tried to pull one of his legs from the mire. He shot a spell at the water. It frothed and foamed, but another powerful, overriding force sucked Semihazah down until he stood waist deep in the puddle.

He thrashed about and tried to pull himself out.

"His spell isn't working," Samuel said. "He can't get out. How's that possible? I saw him levitate above the ectoplasm just moments ago."

"The diamond has him," Hawkwick said, his face pale with fear. "How can the gem have such power?"

"Help me," Semihazah begged. "Hawkwick, try your magic!"

Hawkwick stepped forward and tentatively dipped a finger into the water, then examined the drop on the tip of his finger. "It's ordinary water," he said. "Transform. See if you can turn to shadow and escape. Try."

The demon stopped thrashing and became still; disbelief flickered in his eyes. "I can't transform," he said pathetically. "The diamond is draining my power."

A shocked look crossed Hawkwick's face, and he edged back as if he suddenly saw his own fate in what was happening to Semihazah.

"My friend," Semihazah implored. "Don't

desert me now. I'm afraid. I never thought I'd face . . . *this*."

"But what happens to me if I stay?" Hawkwick said and twirled into a gust of smoke.

In retaliation, Semihazah lifted his hand. Power arced from his palm, and the air ruptured with a violent release of energy. A gust of wind stormed about, chasing Hawkwick. His shadow skated up over the craggy walls and disappeared into the tunnel.

"Man, if that's his power when it's drained, then what must it be like when he's fully charged?" Obie asked.

Semihazah screamed, and his magic exploded, shaking the cavern. The ground trembled beneath Berto's feet. Fissures opened overhead, spilling pebbles.

"Help me," Semihazah pleaded. His mouth stretched open in agony as his chin hit the dirty water. A high-pitched and mournful cry escaped his lips before the mud percolated and covered his head.

Berto stared in horror, almost pitying the

demon, and at the same time wondering at the power of the diamond.

"The tunnel's collapsing," Kyle yelled. "We need to get everyone out."

Berto ran with his roommates to the edge of the pit. "The gold bands strangle them when they stop working," Berto said. "We'll have to remove their shackles before we can rescue them."

"I still remember the spell I used to take off the band around Maddie's neck," Obie said. He started writing runic letters, repeating the same incantation over and over.

"Courtney!" Berto yelled.

"Berto?" she said, recognizing his voice. She looked up. A silly smile curled on her lips, and she seemed to forget her pain. "Berto, you're naked."

"Is this really everyone's big concern?" Berto grumbled as he wrapped the cape around his body. "Tell them to trust me."

"Are you kidding?" Pete asked, working his fingers into his tightening collar. "We don't need anyone to tell us to trust you. You're the gatekeeper at Quake. We all know you."

Berto made a mental promise to himself. He didn't care what his boss said about the way Pete looked. From now on, every time Pete showed up at Quake, Berto was letting him inside.

"We're going to take the shackles off your necks," Berto shouted, hoping everyone could hear him over the cascading rocks and sand. "But before we do, we need to have you hold on to each other, so you'll have a connection to me and be able to see. Without a talisman or a guide, outsiders see only mists here."

The kids nearest him seemed to understand; Berto sensed that they had all experienced the mists when they had first entered Nefandus.

"All right, then." Berto leaned over and grabbed Courtney's hand. She linked arms with Pete. Soon everyone was connected, and Obie sent the incantations flying. Shackles fell with a loud clatter. Kids shouted, applauded, and whooped, happy to be free.

Minutes later, they were stumbling into the

tunnel. Berto felt a surge of relief, hoping he could save everyone now.

He plunged forward, holding Courtney's hand and blindly leading the way. His feet landed on jagged rocks, but he ignored the pain. Then, without warning, he collided with a barrier.

"No!" he yelled, and, using his free hand, he patted the wall, searching for another opening.

"What's wrong?" Courtney asked.

"We're trapped," Berto admitted.

CHAPTER TWENTY-SEVEN

SUDDEN BRIGHTNESS stung Berto's eyes. Runic letters glowed above him, throwing off sparks.

"I'll get us out," Obie said. He whispered a ritual chant before he released the magic words. The incantation bored into the ground. Loud, deep thunder rumbled through the earth and jolted the cavern. Rocks and dirt began to slide.

Kids cried out for help.

But then the deep, rolling sound stopped,

and dim starlight glimmered in the darkness. Obie had broken through the barricade. "Hurry," he shouted.

Berto led the others outside. He found his clothes near one of the bare trees and stepped into his jeans, awkwardly pulling them on using only one hand. He felt someone staring at him and glanced up.

A line of girls, their arms interlinked, stood together watching him.

He caught Obie's insolent smile.

"Promise me you'll make everyone forget this moment," Berto said.

"We've got visitors!" Kyle yelled, interrupting him.

Thunderheads gathered on the horizon, blacker than the night. The dark clouds twisted together, rolling toward them with incredible speed.

Sudden terror ripped through Berto.

"Regulators," he whispered, turning slowly and searching the horizon. "Which way do we go to find a portal?"

"I've got someone who can show us,"

Samuel said. He touched the delicate stone carving of a raven that hung around his neck.

A loud, harsh *caw* disturbed the silence, and a raven soared above them, its glossy wings catching the crimson starlight. It circled overhead before gliding toward the evergreen trees.

"Follow it!" Samuel shouted.

Within a few moments, they were running under thick boughs, holding hands and linking arms to form a human chain. The scent of pine filled their lungs, a welcome relief from the dirt-clogged air inside the tunnel.

When they reached the crest of the hill, everyone looked over the edge of a cliff down at jutting black rocks and tide pools. The wind lashed around them, seeming to pull them forward.

"We must be on a peninsula," Obie said. He gazed up into the sky to find the raven.

"We found the portal," Samuel said with authority. "This is the same one I used to escape. That means we have to ask everyone to trust us again and dive off the cliff."

Courtney looked at Berto and tightened her hold on his hand. "I won't hesitate this time," she said. "I promise."

"None of us will," Pete added, looking slightly dizzy as he stepped back from the ledge. "We want to get out of here."

Everyone seemed to agree. Berto didn't detect unwillingness or even a tremor of fear in anyone's face; they all wanted to go home.

"But how will we know when the portal is open?" Berto asked.

As if in reply, the raven swooped down, and when it neared the rocks it disappeared.

"It's open now," Samuel said excitedly.

"I'll go first and wait on the other side," Obie whispered. "Then as they come through I'll cast a spell to make them forget where they've been."

"Can you do so many?" Kyle asked, trying hard not to be overheard.

"I'll try my best," Obie said and took Courtney's hand, changing places with Berto and assuming the lead.

"How are we ever going to explain all this?" Berto asked.

"If my magic is strong enough, we won't have to," Obie countered, and then he marked the air with a symbol for good luck and dove off the cliff, pulling Courtney with him. Pete yelled as he tumbled after them. No one broke the chain.

Berto and Kyle brought up the rear to make sure no stragglers were left stranded in the churning mists.

"How did you know to come here to rescue me?" Berto asked Kyle.

"Piya told us you needed help," Kyle said. "We went to Semihazah's mansion first, and then to the dig. We wouldn't have been able to find you except that Piya had been eavesdropping and knew where Hawkwick had been holding the kidnapped kids."

"Did she go back to the loft?" Berto asked, anxious to thank her.

"She's probably back at Hawkwick's apartment," Kyle said. "She wanted to stay in Nefandus and keep up her charade with

Hawkwick in case things went wrong and we got caught. If that had happened she was going to try to free us."

"She didn't think it through," Berto said. "I'm going after Piya."

"I'll come with you," Kyle offered.

"Stay," Berto said. "Obie and Samuel need your help."

Berto threw himself into the air. His body spread out, transforming as he started back toward town. He sped across the countryside, a pitch-black stream of smoke, gliding close to the ground as the cloud of Regulators streamed over him, heading for the portal. But Berto knew they were already too late.

Berto landed on the stairs in front of Hawkwick's apartment. Black specks of shadow swirled in front of him as he struggled to pull his body back together. His long, hard physical effort had left him weak, and he knew he wouldn't be able to transform again for a while.

At last he materialized and opened the door. As soon as he stepped inside, he sensed that something was different. Sadness shrouded the evil tension that had existed in the rooms before. He hoped the sorrow wasn't coming from Piya.

He crept through the hallway to the library. Hawkwick stood in the center of the room, covered with dirt. Piya was staring up at him.

"You've disappointed me, Piya," Hawkwick said with a heavy sigh. He dropped into a chair, seeming depleted. "Your treachery has cost me everything."

"I couldn't let you harm Berto," she replied.

Berto entered the room before Hawkwick could respond.

An astonished look crossed Hawkwick's face, followed by a thin smile. "What is it inside you that makes you risk so much for others?" Hawkwick said tiredly.

Berto glanced at Piya. "She sacrificed everything for me," he said. "I wouldn't be able to live with myself if I didn't try to save her now."

Hawkwick nodded, but a terrible sadness seemed to hold him, and for the briefest moment Berto sensed that Hawkwick was grieving for his old friend Semihazah. Could Followers mourn and have bonds of friendship? He hadn't thought so.

"And Semihazah?" Hawkwick asked.

"He's gone," Berto answered; suddenly he understood. Hawkwick was alone now, without anyone.

"I'll miss my friend," Hawkwick said. He lifted his hand, but instead of casting a spell, he waved Berto and Piya away.

Berto hesitated, afraid it was a trick, but when Hawkwick didn't try to stop them, he grabbed Piya's hand and swung her into his arms. He carried her from the room.

"You're covered with dirt," Piya said and ran a finger over his lips.

"I'll take a shower when we're back at the loft," Berto answered. "But don't get the wrong idea about what I'm doing. We're friends."

"Then put me down," she said petulantly. "I can walk."

Berto gently let her go, and then together they sped down the long, winding stairs. The sound of their footsteps on the iron staircase brought Followers to their windows and balconies.

"Ignore them," Piya said confidently as she and Berto walked down the twisting street. "They hate Hawkwick. He's offended them too often. They'll applaud our escape. We only have to worry about Regulators."

When they'd gotten one block further, the air trembled as if her words had summoned a patrol of Regulators. Pale blue sparks crackled over the eaves and down the side of the building ahead of them; then shadows fluttered around the pinnacles and spires.

Berto pulled Piya against him, realizing his mistake. "Hawkwick let us go because he had already summoned the Regulators," Berto said, and started to inch back. But more shadows gathered behind them and grew denser. Hands formed, followed by twisted, angry faces.

"I'm sorry, Piya," Berto said and kissed the top of her head.

"Sorry about what?" she asked. She seemed unaware of the danger.

"I should have been more cautious," he answered. "I can't fight so many."

"You're forgetting something," she said, flashing him her pixie smile. "Hawkwick taught me how to pass into the earth realm without using a portal."

She took his hand, and velvet softness enveloped him. His vision blurred until the street disappeared. The familiar membrane wrapped itself around him, and then his body became numb as his atoms rearranged for the earth realm.

They landed on the beach.

Berto rested in the hot sand. But instead of the soothing crash of waves, it was Kyle's voice that he heard, amplified though a microphone. He jumped up.

Kyle stood nearby, in front of a group of reporters, his hair matted and dirty; he was still wearing the same pajama bottoms he'd had on earlier.

"The happening was a way to make people think about how much they would miss the ones they loved if something did take them away,"

Kyle said loudly, evidently trying to put passion into his words.

Up and down the beach kids from the pit were hugging their parents, talking to police officers, and posing for news cameras.

Obie waved and rushed over to join Berto and Piya.

"What did you do?" Berto asked.

"The kidnap victims don't remember much," Obie said. "They think they took part in one of Kyle's artistic performances. Kyle is probably going to be put on probation for pulling a prank like this." Obie winked and wagged his finger. "But I'm still casting spells." Then he saw someone. "Got to go. The mayor and city council members just arrived, and I definitely need to make them see the humor in all of this."

"Good luck," Piya said.

Berto glanced down at the dirt encrusting his body. He ran into the water and dove under a wave.

When he broke through the surface, Piya surprised him. She had splashed into the water next to him, and she wrapped her arms around his neck.

"Don't tell me you're still committed to Ashley," she whispered, and kissed him softly.

He tasted the salt water on her lips, and a pleasant chill swept through him. The world seemed suddenly good again.

CHAPTER TWENTY-EIGHT

ARKNESS FELL across L.A. as the moon eclipsed the sun. People lined Wilshire Boulevard, wearing welder's caps and holding solar filter glass in front of their eyes. Traffic had stopped, and drivers climbed from their cars to experience the night sun.

Berto left his friends and hurried inside the Los Angeles County Museum of Art. He showed his ticket to the guard and took the steps two at a time. He needed to know what had happened to Ashley, and he sensed he'd find his answer there.

He approached the ancient bas-relief panel, and a sense of awe overwhelmed him. The artwork had changed. He lovingly placed his hand on a likeness of Ashley. Carved with dramatic detail, she stood between the king and his sentinel.

Ashley's arms were wrapped around the king's shoulders, her smile mysterious and enchanting. Berto's heart ached for her. He pressed his forehead against the cold stone wishing he could hold her again. How many times had she promised to make him a king if he would journey back to Mesopotamia with her? He wondered if she had worked her charms on the ruler to become his queen, or if she had used her power to make him become the king.

"I hope you had a good life, Ashley," he whispered, and then he turned, feeling as if a tremendous burden had been lifted from him. He could look forward to the future again, because while in the Akashic Records he had caught a glimpse of his own fate: he had met his destined love.

He walked back outside and found Piya sitting with his friends around a table on the plaza. She smiled up at Berto as he approached, shading her eyes from the sun that once again blazed brightly.

Piya sat between Kyle and Obie. Maddie and Samuel were sharing a salad. Even Courtney was there, along with Tabitha and Ana.

"Berto," Maddie called. "Why didn't you stay and watch the eclipse? It was unbelievable."

He studied Maddie with a curiosity that made her tilt her head and give him a questioning look. He wasn't sure when he'd tell his friends what he had learned about her from the Akashic Records. Then again, maybe he'd keep his secret. It would be more fun to watch Samuel, Kyle, and Obie find out for themselves.

LYNNE EWING is a screenwriter who also counsels troubled teens. In addition to writing all of the Sons of the Dark books, she is the author of the popular companion series Daughters of the Moon. Ms. Ewing lives in Los Angeles, California.